IT'S HARD TO KNOW WHERE YOU'LL END UP:

… in a sulky race,
    trotting against the best horses in the county.

… in the stable,
    watching your horse give birth to a foal.

… in a polo match,
    smashing the ball between the goal posts.

What happens in this book is up to you, according to the choices you make, page by page. You'll find over thirty possible endings, from scary to silly to surprising. And it all starts when your parents give you a very special birthday present.…

D1328698

A HORSE NAMED FUNNY BITS

ROSE MARIE GOBLE

Chariot Books

Chariot Books is an imprint of David C. Cook Publishing Co.

David C. Cook Publishing Co., Elgin, Illinois 60120
David C. Cook Publishing Co., Weston, Ontario

A HORSE NAMED FUNNY BITS
© 1983 by Rose Marie Goble for the text and John Hayes for the illustrations
Book and series design by Ray Cioni/The Cioni Artworks
Cover design by Mark Duebner

Printed in the United States of America
89 88 87 86 85 84 83   5 4 3 2 1

ISBN 0-89191-787-X
LC 83-72505

CAUTION!

This is not a normal book! If you read it straight through, it won't make any sense.

Instead, you must start at page 1 and then turn to the pages where your choices lead you. Your first decision is which horse to buy. After that, you're holding the reins! What will you do with your new horse? The choice is up to you.

If you want to read this book, you must choose to
Turn to page 1.

"Surprise! We are giving you a horse for your birthday!"

You cannot believe you have heard your father correctly. Your very own horse, a dream you never thought would come true. This is truly a birthday you will never forget. The whole family—Mom, Dad, and your little brother, Tommy—is going with you to the Valley View Stables to pick out your horse.

When you arrive at the horse farm, you are amazed at all the drab brown horses. Disappointment fills you. You didn't want just any old horse. Looking around you see a large white horse in a corral.

"That one," you tell your father as you point across the fence.

"The white stallion is not for sale," says the owner.

Father asks you again, "Which one do you want?"

You shake your head. "I don't want any of these. I want a palomino, an Appaloosa, or a pinto."

"Those are in high demand," the man says sadly. "I don't have but one each in my stable." He turns, and you follow him.

The stable smells horsey and has loose straw poking out of the corners. He leads you past so many empty stalls that you wonder if there are enough horses in the world to fill them. Finally he pauses in front of a closed door. You watch breathlessly and are not disappointed again.

Turn to page 2.

"Here is my only palomino." He indicates the largest and most beautiful horse you have ever seen. He brings it out of the stall so you can get a better look. The golden coat gleams in the light; all four legs have white stockings from their shins down to their hooves. The mane and tail are a creamy color. You walk up to it and reach out to pet the white stripe down its nose. The man quickly grabs your hand.

"This horse is not as gentle as the others," he warns. "She is a champion and schooled for the show ring. You may not be experienced enough to handle this one." He continues to stand between you and the horse who tosses her head impatiently. Then the owner leads the golden beauty back into the stall.

Choices: You decide to take the palomino (turn to page 6).

You decide to look at a few other horses (turn to page 138).

He leads you through two empty corrals to a small shed. Inside he turns on a light, and you see a very ragged horse. "She is my only Appaloosa at the present time."

"What's wrong with her?" you ask. "Her ribs are showing and she's dirty."

"She's old, and her teeth are bad. She can only eat ground grain, which is quite expensive. I'm going to sell her for dog food."

"Oh, no!" you exclaim. You cannot bear to think of any horse being made into dog food.

"If you are interested in buying her," the man continues, "you will find that she is a real bargain. She's going to have a foal in a couple of months."

A foal! How exciting! Then you would have two horses.

Choices: You choose the Appaloosa mare and save her life (turn to page 8).
You choose the palomino show horse to make your name famous and rich (turn to page 6).
You choose the friendly pinto, a Shetland cow pony (turn to page 7).

The western movie is sensational. The boy and girl capture a beautiful, wild palamino. But rustlers steal the beautiful stallion from them. You are happy when the girl and boy solve the mystery and lead the posse to the rustlers and the herd of horses they have stolen during the last months.

The lights of the theater come on, and you rise to leave.

"Wait," says Albert. "Let's get some popcorn and see the other feature. After all, we've already paid for it."

"What is it?"

"Oh, I don't know, but they're always super. I know you'll like it."

You really want to go home, but you stay and watch it anyway. It's a first-class horror movie that makes you close your eyes. Even then the music and sound effects drive shivers up your spine. When it's over, you walk home as dark shadows dance around the alley and every object seems ready to pounce on you.

THE END

You watch proudly as the palomino steps daintily into the horse van. You climb into the front seat with your father. He drives the car out of the drive and then turns to talk to you as you go home.

"Happy birthday. The responsibility of feeding, watering, grooming, and exercising the palomino is yours. It must be done every day. His stable area must be kept dry and clean. It's a big job, but I know that you can do it. Should you have any questions, just ask me."

You hum a jaunty tune. You know that you can care for the palomino, since you've been reading about horses for a long time. Your neighbor has a series of small jumps in his yard. You know he would let you use them to see if the palomino's been jumped before. It's a warm thought that brings a smile on your face.

Then you think of your friend Alvin who also has a horse. He invited you to come over and ride sometime. You know from previous visits that his home is on the very outskirts of town, and there are a thousand or more places to ride horses and have lots of fun.

Your father pulls the van into the yard and backs it up to a small hill. You pop out and undo the van doors, swinging them wide open so the horse—Funny Bits—will have plenty of room. The horse quietly backs out of the van, and you take her into the shed. Now you know that she is yours.

Choices: You ride the jumps (turn to page 11).
You ride to Alvin's (turn to page 9).

"Can I ride the pinto since I'm going to keep her?"

"Sure," says the owner.

Immediately you open the gate and bring the pinto out by pulling on her forelock. She follows you easily, and you wiggle onto her back. You lean over her neck, just like the stable owner has taught you, and guide her outside. The horse goes only so far and doubles back to the stable. Quickly you turn her around. The pinto, Funny Bits, shows a mind of her own. She turns a complete circle and heads for the stable door.

"Here," says the man, bringing a bridle. "You can control her with this." He slips the bit between the pony's teeth and the leather headstall behind the short, fuzzy ears. Then he hands the reins to you. The pony chomps the bit, slobbering a little. "That's how she got the name Funny Bits."

"She is funny," you say. "I like riding her."

"Let me ride," says Tommy, running up to you.

You stare down at him. You have not had your horse for five minutes, and he wants to ride it. You know that once he's on the horse he will not want to get off. On top of that, you will have to lead the horse while he rides. Funny Bits is too small to ride double.

"Please let me ride."

You love your little brother a lot, but you're not quite sure how much right now.

Choices: You let him ride (turn to page 12).
You decide to continue riding yourself (turn to page 13).

As your father begins to write out the check to pay for your horse, he asks, "Do you want to leave the mare here until the foal is born, or shall we take her home?"

"Let's leave her here," says your mother immediately. "This man has had more experience in bringing foals into the world and feeding undernourished mother horses."

"Please understand," says your father, looking straight into your eyes, "you do not have to leave her here. This is your horse and your responsibility. What do you want to do?"

Again you look at your mare. She is definitely very bony, but her stomach bulges. You shiver when you think of something going wrong, and yet you really want to show your best friend your new horse. A few months is a very long time.

"Whether you leave the horse here or take her," says the stable owner, turning to you, "I will give you a book that suggests the proper food and exercise. It also tells you how to deliver foals, but you should get the help of a vet."

He goes to a drawer, pulls out a book, and gives it to you. You flip through the pages.

Choices: You decide to take the horse home (turn to page 15).

You decide to leave the mare in the stable until the colt is born (turn to page 16).

Your friend runs to meet you as you ride your horse into his yard. "Boy, you sure picked a winner," he says. Alvin knows all about horses even if he is your age. "She has strong legs and an intelligent face. If the intelligence is there, you can do anything with a horse."

You nod and smile. Then you notice his little sister and brother standing on the porch. They admire Funny Bits, too.

"Say, let's ride to Duff's, OK?" asks Alvin.

"Sure!" you exclaim. "Let's go."

"Well, give me time to saddle up."

Duff has taught both of you to ride. He is also a good friend and your Sunday school teacher. You know he would like to see your new horse.

"Can we go, too?" chorus two small voices.

You look startled. You turn to ask Alvin, and he shrugs his shoulders.

Choices: You take Alvin's brother and sister with you (turn to page 18).
You decide they cannot go with you and Alvin (turn to page 19).

You strike out. Your team loses the game that day, because you are a poor team captain. As you walk home, you realize that baseball is not your game.

"I'm going to be a horseman and raise beautiful horses," you tell your friend.

"You'll make more home runs with a horse under you than on any baseball diamond," agrees your friend. "I'm going home."

"Well, I'm going to visit Funny Bits."

At home you find Funny Bits rested and willing to take you on a short ride. You saddle up and walk to the park. The trees cast leafy shadows to keep you and Funny Bits cool. You stop long enough to get acquainted with the pond. After a small drink, you quietly ride home. As you devote more and more time to Funny Bits, you definitely know that your baseball life has come to **THE END.**

You have to pull hard to raise yourself into the palomino's saddle. She is a large horse. She moves around as you struggle, but it doesn't scare you much. Once you begin to ride, you suddenly realize how powerful your horse is. When she trots, you flop all over the saddle so you give her more rein. Funny Bits begins to canter, and you are amazed at the speed. Wind brushes the mane into your eyes. It's exciting, but you're a little scared.

Funny Bits runs out into the pasture as if she knows you want to jump some hurdles. She starts moving faster, and you lean forward over her neck. Quickly you come towards a small fence. Her back feet thrust you both into the air like the jets on a rocket. Now the fence is below you, and you know you are flying. Your horse lands very hard on the other side. You lose your balance and flip right over her head. She snorts, jumps again, but never touches you.

You get up. In a daze you brush sticks, leaves, and grass from your clothes. Funny Bits is standing nearby.

"Easy, girl," you say as you slowly walk up to her with your hand stretched outward. She watches you closely but does not move. You pet her nose.

"Good horse," you tell her as you take both reins in your hands.

Choices: You decide to get on and try again **(turn to page 20).**
You decide to walk back to the stable **(turn to page 21).**

You lead Funny Bits around while little brother rides and rides.

"This is fun," he says. "I'm a real cowboy!"

"Really," you mutter. Around and around the yard you go. He never seems to get tired.

"Come on. It's time to go," your father says. "Lead Funny Bits into the van."

Your little brother slides to the ground and runs to your mother. You would like one last ride before getting into the van, so you jump onto the pinto's back and ride her up to the van.

"Thanks for letting Tommy ride," says Mother. "Your pony is so gentle that you could start a pony ride business and earn money."

You think about that. You would earn quite a lot of money, for there are many kids on your block who would gladly pay to ride. But then, both you and Funny Bits would be too tired to ride on your own. Still, if you had money, you could buy a new saddle and some other items you have been dreaming about. The thought is nice, but you wanted to be a professional roper ever since you saw a performing cowboy in a school assembly. You know it will take a lot of time to become handy with a rope. Humm. This decision is difficult.

Choices: You decide to start a pony ride business (turn to page 22).
You decide to learn how to rope calves and become a cowboy (turn to page 24).

Funny Bits is so smart, you decide to teach her some tricks. First, you get her to come when you whistle. She learns to say "Yes" by nodding her head up and down. When you hold up a hoop, she jumps through. Then she learns to bow.

"I saw a horse count to ten," says your best friend who has come to see Funny Bits.

"So what? I saw a horse add, subtract, divide, and multiply," brags your little brother.

"Ah, a horse can't do that," your best friend scoffs.

"He can, too," maintains Tommy. "The man on tv showed how the horse knew the answers."

"If that horse could do it, Funny Bits can, too."

Choices: You decide to please your little brother and teach your horse to be a mathematician (turn to page 25). You decide to teach him to shake hands instead (turn to page 27).

14

Every Tuesday you ride the bus to your grandmother's. She gives you money for watering her lawn, vacuuming her rugs, and running little errands to the nearest store.

On Wednesdays you help your neighbor. Sometimes he wants you to weed his garden, buy him a paper from the corner drugstore, help him wash windows, or wax his car.

Thursdays you ride Funny Bits to deliver newspapers. On Saturday afternoon you often baby-sit your cousins. It is hard work, but you like the pay.

On your days off, you play with Funny Bits and her colt. The colt is growing into a beautiful and well-mannered horse because of your careful attention and care.

Every coin and dollar you make goes into a bank on your bureau. You watch the bank get fuller each week. Soon there will be enough to purchase that new saddle.

Then your Sunday school teacher explains tithing to you and your class on Sunday morning. You learn that God expects all Christians to pay him a tenth of their earnings. You look worriedly at your bank when you get home.

**Choices: You decide to tithe (turn to page 79).
You decide to buy the saddle first (turn to page 82).**

You name the horse Funny Bits as you go home with your horse neighing in the van behind the car. You bed her down in the shed, which your father has refurbished as a stable. Fresh straw covers the floor. Behind it is a fenced lot full of green grass.

Your best friend and two other kids come over when they see the horse van pull into your driveway. They stay and follow you around.

The Appaloosa mare quietly walks into the shed. You run to get the ground grain that the man told you to feed her. Your friends stretch the garden hose across the yard and help you fill a half barrel with cool, clean water. You notice how much dirt and hanging hair is on her. You take your new currycomb and begin to run it over her sides to pull out the dirty hair.

"Can I help?" asks your best friend, petting the soft, velvet nose of the horse. You hand him a brush, and he begins working. You find combing out all those ugly mats takes time and lots of energy.

"Can we help, too?" "Can we ride her?" "What did you name her?" Everyone is shouting out questions. You begin to feel very pressured. You remember reading that new pets need peace and quiet to get used to their new home.

**Choices: You tell them to quit bothering you and your horse (turn to page 47).
You tell them to wait until Saturday for a ride (turn to page 41).**

The stable owner smiles at your decision. "You must meet Malford," he says. "Malford is the wisest man I know when it comes to horses. He knows all the answers."

The owner takes you out of the stable to a small, silver horse trailer hooked to a blue pickup truck. There is a matching silver camper on the pickup. The man knocks staccatolike, and a small person opens the door. You would think he was a boy except his chin has a shadow of beard, and the hair on top of his head is thin.

"Malford, meet the new owner of the Appaloosa mare."

Malford reaches around the stable owner to shake your hand. His calloused palm scrapes yours, and he pumps your arm up and down vigorously. You are amazed at the strength of this short man. His bright eyes seem to glisten unnaturally.

"The Appaloosa mare!" exclaims Malford. "Why I brought her into the world as a filly. I sure do know all about her."

He leaves his trailer and walks back with you to talk about the mare. His legs are bowed as if he's had rickets, but his stride is rhythmic. You find yourself trying to copy it. He winks, embarrassing you.

Choices: You hire Malford to work with your mare (turn to page 31).
You distrust the man (turn to page 33).

Alvin and you ride side by side so you can talk. His little brother's and sister's ponies walk ahead of you.

"How're you making money this year for church camp?" you ask. Every year as far back as you can remember, Alvin has earned his own way. "Since my folks bought me Funny Bits, I have to earn my own camp fee this year."

He nods in an understanding way. "Mom said she'd pay mine this year if I watch the kids all summer."

"Oh." This catches you by surprise. You were counting on his help to raise the money you need.

You ride along for several feet, listening to the horses' hooves crunch leaves on the path.

"You could set up pony rides," he suggests, "or maybe run errands like a pony express."

You grin. "Thanks, Alvin. You're a real pal."

You wonder how much you would have to charge to make enough for the camp fee. With pony rides the customers would have to come to you. How could you advertise to get enough customers? Door to door would be about the only way to find enough errands to run. Either one will be work.

"Come on, Alvin, let's canter for a while."

He nods, and you are off.

Choices: **You decide to set up pony rides (turn to page 22).**
You decide to run errands (turn to page 113).

Alvin's mother promptly comes to the door. "If Alvin goes, he has to take the kids. I need him to watch them for me today."

He looks at you, and you nod.

"Yea!" the kids yell in unison.

You groan.

"I'll saddle Sissy's horse if you'll saddle the other," suggests Alvin.

Once both horses are saddled, you mount. All four horses start off in a mob, but this changes when you and Alvin fall behind and let the two ponies lead.

"Ever try polo?" Alvin asks you.

"No."

"Well, neither have I, but Duff was telling me last Sunday after church that he used to play. In fact, he said he would set goals up in his field so we can have a game if we want."

"Perfect," you declare. "Let's go."

"Ahhhhh!" Alvin's sister screams as her pony rears back and throws her. Something has spooked the usually gentle pony. The pony turns and runs.

Choices: **You ride after the pony (turn to page 37).**
You stop to help the little girl (turn to page 38).

Funny Bits dances about, but you finally climb back into the saddle. Elated by your success, you touch her lightly on the neck. "Come on, girl, Let's try that again. This time I'm going to stay on."

You are right. The next time you do manage to hang on. After a while you discover the knack of helping your mount over the jumps and landing gracefully with her. You keep an even pressure on the reins and hold Funny Bits to a slow canter until her body is in line with the jump. Slowly, as you judge the distance, you let out your hands and feel Funny Bits's strides lengthen. With perfect rhythm she reaches the jump and leaps skyward. This time you are ready. You lean forward and fly with her—no longer a lump of clay, but almost a part of the horse.

Now for the real challenge! You raise each of the jumps an inch higher. Funny Bits seems to have no trouble jumping any of them. You ride over them a second time to make sure. The height is easy for her, so you raise the jumps again. She takes each one with finesse.

Funny Bits is a good jumper. You are so proud of her that you want others to see how well she can jump.

Choices: **You decide to enter a jumping con-test (turn to page 39).**
You decide to go fox hunting with Funny Bits (turn to page 42).

As you walk back to the stable, leading a very docile Funny Bits, you decide that you will never ride her again. You tell yourself that actually you weren't scared, but you had placed yourself and Funny Bits in a dangerous position. Jumping is not a safe hobby for people or horses. You were lucky not to break an arm or leg. And horses have had to be shot because of serious injury. You shudder at the thought. Poor, beautiful Funny Bits!

Then you see a horse show on television. Each horse is perfectly groomed. Great! You can do that. You watch the person handling the horse in the ring. Would it be best to hire a professional to work with Funny Bits, or could you do it yourself?

You watch Funny Bits happily grazing in the grassy lot that evening. Maybe your horse would lead the happiest life right here in this pasture. You wish Funny Bits could talk and tell you what she'd rather do.

Choices: **You put Funny Bits out to pasture (turn to page 44).**
You hire a professional to show Funny Bits (turn to page 45).

You nail this sign on your front gate:

PONY RIDES
25¢
Right After School Every Night

Funny Bits becomes very popular in the neighborhood. When the wind blows down your sign, you really don't have to replace it. Still you put up a bigger and better looking one. Some mothers hire you to bring Funny Bits to birthday parties to entertain the children. You realize the adults trust you and Funny Bits.

One evening after you've hung up the bridle and fed Funny Bits, you spread your earnings out on the kitchen table to count.

"Mom! Guess what!" you call to her in excitement. "There's enough money to buy that new saddle."

"Very good, dear. Have you been tithing your money?"

Tithing? "But isn't tithing only for older people?"

Mom shakes her head, and you know without doubt that God expects one-tenth of all the money lying on the table.

"But there's only enough to buy the saddle."

Your mom puts a hand on your shoulder. "Remember you are earning money to go to church camp, too."

"In time I'll have enough for that," you say, thinking only of the saddle.

Choices: **You decide to tithe (turn to page 79).**
You decide to buy the saddle anyway (turn to page 82).

24

You ride Funny Bits every day. Mother gives you a bit of clothesline to practice roping. Your loops sag, but you throw them at fence posts anyway, trying to learn to rope the post. One day your father comes out to watch you.

"See how well I am doing," you brag.

"Your slipknot could use some adjusting," he says. You let him show you how to retie it.

A week later a friend of yours comes over to watch and ride Funny Bits. While he rides, you continue to throw the rope. You still cannot rope anything, but now your rope always hits the object you aim at.

"You have the wrong kind of rope," says your friend. "Cowboys use a stiff hemp rope called a lariat."

"Really?"

Choices: You trust your friend's judgment and buy a lariat (turn to page 46).
You decide to purchase a bola, like one you've read about in a South American novel (turn to page 77).

"Now what's the trick?" you ask your little brother.

Tommy grins as if he won't ever tell you the secret. But once he realizes you think he is bluffing, he begins to talk. "The man did the math in his head," he explains. "The horse simply stomped its foot every time the man patted his leg."

"Ah, I knew it!" you exclaim. "All we have to do is teach Funny Bits to paw the ground at a certain signal."

That night while you are eating supper your little brother taps his spoon on his plate. Suddenly you know how to teach Funny Bits the trick.

"I'll buy one of those fancy show sticks and tap the ground," you tell your brother.

With your brother's help, Funny Bits learns the trick rapidly. You work every day until the act is perfect. Your mother makes three capes: one for you, one for Tommy, and one for Funny Bits. She embroiders "The Horse Genius, Funny Bits" on all of them.

Your brother wears his cape to school to advertise your new act. Thirty-seven kids watch the first performance. The three of you become so popular that you are asked to perform at fairs, garage sales, and even in a circus sideshow.

One day you decide you are too old for such foolishness and give Funny Bits to your little brother. Your act has come to **THE END!**

"We are going to have an outdoor Nativity musical this year," the choir director announces.

You sit up in excitement. "Does that mean live animals, a stable, and costumes, too?"

"It surely does," he says. "A farmer is bringing two tame sheep and his cow."

"All right!" exclaims everyone but you. You are thinking. The director hands out parts: Mary, Joseph, several angels, shepherds, wise men, and a stable owner. You are the stable owner.

"We'll sing most of the old favorites, but I want you to learn a few new ones," he continues. "We'll have microphones and amplifiers so everyone listening will enjoy it."

You have a question. "Do you have a donkey?"

"No."

"Could Funny Bits have that part?"

Your friends laugh, but the director answers, "Certainly."

In the next few weeks you practice with the choir and with Funny Bits at home. It is hard work, but Funny Bits responds fantastically. The night of the play she is a tremendous success. People from the audience commend you on her acting ability. You agree that she is a wonder horse, but you are glad the show has come to **THE END!**

Funny Bits becomes very stubborn when you try to teach her to shake hands. She steps on your hands, butts you with her head, and learns to nibble your fingers. You know that nibbling could lead to biting, so you give the idea second thoughts.

"What else can we do to entertain ourselves?" you ask your friend as he is about to leave.

"Well, only one can ride at a time," he says. "Riding's fun, but waiting for a turn is boring."

"I know. We need to improve the system." You chew a piece of grass. "I know. Let's make her an Indian pony. She can carry the burdens when we move our village from place to place."

"Then nobody gets to ride," objects your friend. "Maybe we could hitch her to a wagon. That way lots of us could ride at the same time."

You think your idea is great, but your friend's has a lot of merit, too.

Choices: You decide to play Indian (turn to page 49).
You decide to hitch Funny Bits up to a wagon (turn to page 52).

Finally everyone arrives at Duff's house. Duff collects you all together in his yard under a shady tree to explain polo. "The game comes from Tibet where it was played way back in 600 B.C. Great strength is not as necessary as good horsemanship and an excellent horse."

"What do you mean?" asks Alvin's brother.

Duff turns to you. "Funny Bits has speed and stamina, which are needed in polo. But you have not ridden him as long as Alvin's brother has ridden his pony. That means you will be equal players. You have the faster mount, and he knows his horse better."

Duff continues. "We don't have enough to play a regular game, but Sissy and I will team up against all three of you."

"Yeaaa!" you all shout. The makeshift goals are a pair of posts on either end of the field. You are to hit a soccer ball between the posts to score a point. Duff hands each of you a broom as a mallet and explains the rules.

To hit the ball with your broom, you must stand up in the stirrups and lean to one side. Twice you lose your balance and fall off Funny Bits.

"That's enough for today," Duff finally yells. "It's going to take lots of practice before we can really play polo. Let's try again on Saturday."

You wave to Duff as you turn Funny Bits toward home. Duff really cares for each of you. It's great to have him as a friend.

THE END

You go into the house and flop down on the couch. You use the remote control to turn on the tv. Soon your mother comes into the room.

"Tired of your horse already?" she asks.

"Not really," you answer. The look in your mother's eyes tells you she doesn't believe you.

Two nights later your dad comes into the house quite angry. "When was the last time you tended Funny Bits?"

"Last night."

"Last night! You get out there right now."

You jump up and run outside. Funny Bits is out of water so you have to pull the hose out from the house to fill the tank. While you get the feed, the water overflows, and the shed floods.

"It will be dry tomorrow," you tell Funny Bits. You hurry back to the house without laying down dry straw.

The next day your father makes you clean out the shed. "That horse is going to end up with sore feet and go lame."

"Do I have to do it now?" You want to watch the Saturday morning comics first.

"Right after breakfast."

It takes you all morning to grub out the wet shed. You hate the work. Thinking of all the tv you've missed because of the horse, you begin to hate Funny Bits, too.

The next day your parents have to pressure you to do your chores. After another week of this, your dad sells Funny Bits back to the stable. Your stable grubbing days have come to **THE END.**

You currycomb Funny Bits for hours. The matted hair, cakes of mud, and burrs fall to the floor. You brush the horse until her coat looks much better.

"That's a different horse," says your father when he comes into the shed. "I didn't know that you were such a hard worker.

"A thorough, warm bath will accomplish wonders. Let's lead her outside and crosstie her," he suggests. Your father gets two lead ropes and snaps one to either side of her halter. He ties the other ends to a pair of clothesline posts standing two feet apart.

Then you get a soft, bristled brush and a warm bucket of water. Your father brings out his dandruff shampoo. "We'll do her up in style."

You grin. You never knew he was such a great guy. Both of you sing country western songs as you lather Funny Bits. It takes a lot of time, but finally, when Funny Bits is dry, you both are happy with the results. You lead Funny Bits back to her shed.

"I'll help you rake up the floor," your father says, looking at the mess you left in the shed. "But first we need a garbage bag to put it in. I'll go to the house and get one."

Choices: You braid your horse's tail and mane (turn to page 56).
You're so tired you sit on a bale and rest until he returns (turn to page 57).
You decide to surprise your father and rake all the junk into a pile (turn to page 58).

Malford talks constantly; however, his voice seems to soothe you. He follows you back to the Appaloosa mare. "Your mare was born on the Happy A ranch, the most famous of Appaloosa farms. I remember her daddy, Two Bits. He won the grand champion title more than fifteen times!"

"Wow!" you exclaim. "What was her mother's bloodline?" You're proud to use professional breeding terms, but Malford doesn't seem to notice.

"Hmm," he murmurs, "just a minute. I never forget…" His smile has changed into a fierce frown. You start to draw away from him, but then he chuckles. "Now I remember. Her dam was Funny Fanny. That's how she got her name. Funny from Fanny, and Bits from her sire." He slaps his hand against his pant leg. "What a name! Funny Bits!"

When you reach the mare's stall, Malford's mood changes again.

"That Jones! He shouldn't be allowed to own horses, treating an Appaloosa like this. He bought her from Happy A and practically abandoned her. He knows better than to leave a fine horse out all winter in bad pasture."

Turn to page 32.

You are surprised at his anger and try to soothe him. "Well, give us time. We'll fatten her up on lots of ground feed."

"You bet," Malford says. "She'll be beautiful just like before. Just think. She's bred to Spotted Boy. That'll make a splendid foal. Well, I've got to get back to work, kid. Why don't you move along now?"

You do have some homework and chores at home, and you're paying Malford to do the work. But Funny Bits is your horse. You wonder what to do.

Choices: You stay to help Malford (turn to page 34).

You decide to go home (turn to page 36).

You stare at Malford one minute longer. You see evil sparks in the back of his eyes. You cannot trust your mare to him. If he knew so much about horses, why did he allow her to get so dirty and skinny? You decide to take her home.

When you get her to your house, you put fresh straw down in her shed. She sniffs at it gratefully and lies down.

You call the local veterinarian. When his pickup drives into the yard, you go out to meet him and take him to see Funny Bits immediately.

"She's a mite thin, but she's foaled before." He takes out a small notebook. "I'd advise you to add this vitamin supplement to her feed. I don't want you running her or getting her hot and sweaty, but she needs daily exercise. Walk her. Understand?"

You nod.

"She'll probably foal in the middle of the night and surprise you. Call me if there's a problem."

One evening you watch the mare stand up and walk out to a corner of the grassy paddock. Her nose sniffs the ground, but she doesn't eat anything. *That's odd,* you think. *I'd better call the vet in the morning.*

You get up early to check on the mare. When you open the stable door, you notice something dark standing next to her. A foal!

His long legs look too high for the rest of him, but his ears flip forward as you approach. He lets you pet his nose before hiding behind his mother. You're delighted. Your long wait for the colt has successfully reached **THE END.**

Malford makes you muck out stalls, carry water, and clean tack, while he talks about horses.

"Now, kid," he says one day, "Funny Bits will probably have her foal within the next week. Her udder has developed, and the milk is down. On the day of the foaling, she'll become somewhat restless and unfriendly. Then just before birth, she'll steam."

"Steam? What's that?" you ask.

Malford grins. "She'll drip with sweat—worse than if she'd been out plowing in a July noon."

"Then what do we do?"

"You get me fast," says Malford. "I'll handle the foaling. I don't want anything to go wrong!"

When you visit the stable a couple days later, Funny Bits lays her ears back. She acts as if she will bite, and her skin looks shiny.

Choices: **You go tell Malford (turn to page 62).**
You decide Funny Bits has just been heavily exercised (turn to page 64).

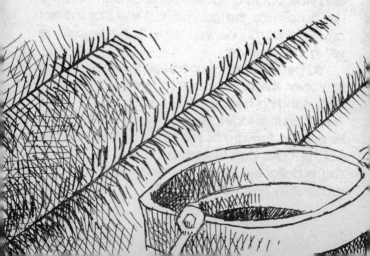

You go into the living room and turn on the tv. "Mystery Theater" is on, and the show's entitled "Horse Thieves." You watch thieves steal thoroughbred colts from stables. You become very infuriated over the stupidity of the owners. They don't realize their employees are substituting dead horses for the thoroughbreds and claiming that the stolen horses have died from disease, foaling, or injury. You think about Malford and the owner of the stable. Over the weeks you've wondered why Malford has seemed hesitant about letting you see Funny Bits, but you've always believed his excuses. He tells you that pregnant mares shouldn't be ridden after the tenth month. Now you think there might be something fishy.

Suddenly your phone rings and you answer it.

"This is Valley View Stable calling," a woman says. "Are you the owner of the Appaloosa mare?"

A woman! In all of your visits to the stables you have only seen Malford and the owner working there.

"Yes, I'm the owner," you answer.

She clears her throat. "I have some very sad news. You must come to the stable immediately. Your mare died while foaling."

You hang up slowly. It is just as you feared.

Choices: **You decide to call the police (turn to page 65).**

You want to solve the mystery yourself, so you call your friend Alvin to help you (turn to page 66).

Funny Bits and you crash through the brush after the runaway. Tree limbs scrape your arms and legs and almost unseat you. Alvin's little brother follows. His pony's nose is right next to Funny Bits's tail.

"Go back," you yell. "I can get him without your help."

The little boy continues to shadow you. You are afraid Funny Bits will kick the pony's nose, and cause the kid to fall off and get hurt. You feel you've had enough trouble without that.

"Alvin needs you to help take your sister home. Go back."

"Find Sissy's horse," he insists.

You decide to ignore him. If he gets hurt, it's his tough luck. Then your conscience bugs you. Sure he'd be the hurt one, but if he got killed, you'd feel guilty for the rest of your life. You stop Funny Bits and slide off to confront the little boy face-to-face.

Choices: **You take him along with you, but you insist on leading his pony (turn to page 110).**
You lead him back to Alvin (turn to page 67).

38

You dismount quickly and check over the little girl. She is more mad than hurt.

"Dirty old horse!" she yells.

"Where do you hurt?" you ask.

She sits up. "I'm not hurt."

"Then what's the matter?"

"I want my horse back." She stops crying and slowly stands up.

"Well, that's better. We'll have to go and catch it. Climb up on Funny Bits, and we'll ride double."

For the first time she smiles. "I like her. She's beautiful."

You both get mounted. Then Alvin arrives, leading his sister's horse. You slide down and reach around to pull her from the saddle.

She is quick. She kicks Funny Bits hard and slaps her with the reins. "Hi, yi yi!" she yells. Funny Bits plunges forward, leaving you standing there.

"Well, of all the ungrateful people," you mutter angrily.

"You can ride hers," offers Alvin.

You consider the small pony thoughtfully.

Choices: You decide to run after Funny Bits (turn to page 68).
You decide to ride her pony (turn to page 69).

You enter Funny Bits in both the Preliminary Jumpers' Class and the Amateur-Owner. The registrar pins a large, white square cloth with the number *28* on your back. "Every contestant must wear identification at all times or be disqualified," he says.

You take a stroll around the ring to look over the jumps before the competition starts. There are five post-and-rail jumps, which look easy. They have two side poles with a bar across that can be adjusted to different heights. The brick wall and the chicken coop are another matter. The brick wall looks real, and you know many horses are afraid to try it. The coop is a solid white wall, about three feet wide. You hope Funny Bits feels brave today. At least she won't be frightened by the brush fences. They look fairly natural.

When the time comes to go into the ring, Funny Bits is ready. You adjust your black velvet, hard hat firmly, straighten your back, and raise your toes. The judge smiles as you come into the ring. You smile, but remember not to relax your form.

Turn to page 40.

The contestant clearing the most jumps without fault wins. You look over the field and feel a confidence mounting inside you. Funny Bits can do it. The judge nods, and you are off. You feel like you're flying about the course. You make good time, but Funny Bits clicked one hind leg on the brick wall. A one-half fault.

"Perfect round," says the judge. The crowd claps. You know he is wrong.

Choices: You accept the perfect score (turn to page 70).

You admit your mistake to the judge (turn to page 71).

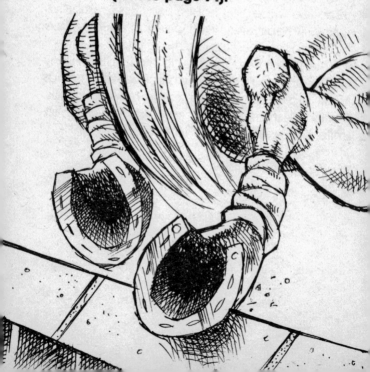

On Saturday morning, you happily jump out of bed, dress, gulp down your breakfast of toast and eggs, and run out to get Funny Bits ready for your friends to ride. You stop on the back porch to glance with pride at your horse. It nickers and comes from the other side of the shed. Her skin is clean from the daily brushing, and it's beginning to shine from the ground-feed diet.

You remove the halter and put it on a peg. Then you hold the bridle before Funny Bits's face and shove the bit between the teeth. Your horse starts chewing as you slide the leather strap over the ears and buckle the strap around the neck.

Saddling is more difficult, but you are learning. Funny Bits stands munching the bit as you lay the thick saddle pad on the back. The saddle is heavy, but the horse accepts it.

"That was the easy part," you say aloud. "Now how do I get that cinch tight?" You pull it with both hands using all the strength in your arms. Funny Bits grunts, and you muster a smile of satisfaction. The cinch strap is snug. Just as you get outside, your friends come running into the yard.

"Can I ride first?" they chorus.

"Quiet!" you order. "I don't want you to frighten Funny Bits." You look the whole group over slowly. You really wanted to ride yourself, but you remember your promise.

Choices: You let them ride first (turn to page 102).

You ride first (turn to page 117).

Bright and early you ride Funny Bits over to a big horse farm. Horses of all shapes and sizes are gathered behind the master of hounds. He sits proud and tall in his red coat. Spotted foxhounds yelp around him.

"This is only a drag hunt, which means that the smell of a fox has been dragged around ahead of us," says your friend. "The hounds will follow that instead of chasing a real fox." Your friend is riding a smaller horse that won't take the jumps as easily as Funny Bits. "Don't worry about me," he says. "I will enjoy myself at the end of the line as much as you will at the front."

You wonder. You know how it feels to always be at the end of the line.

Choices: **You hurry to the front (turn to page 72).**
You decide to ride at the end with your friend (turn to page 73).

44

The lot behind the shed is full of a good grass for Funny Bits to eat and is large enough for her to roll or run at will. Every day you give her fresh water and a ration of oats. Once in a while you offer her a bite of cut-up apple or a chunk of carrot. You remember to keep your palm flat so she won't bite your fingers.

Every Saturday you saddle her so you can ride around the neighborhood and to the park. She has become very fat and sleek. Her hide glows from your daily grooming.

You are careful not to overwork her. Funny Bits has earned a rest. You are content to dream about all of her past accomplishments.

THE END

You telephone the Valley View Stables. "I'd like to hire a professional horse trainer and handler to show my horse," you tell the owner.

"I'll send Malford right over. Malford is the best you can find."

"Thank you." You do not have to wait long after hanging up the phone. The doorbell rings, and there stands a very short and slender man. His long fingers are twisting a cloth cap into pretzels.

"I'm Malford from the stables," he says. "What can I do for you?"

"Are you a professional horse handler?"

"I am the best jockey, showman, trainer, and horse handler on this side of the Mississippi," he says confidently. "Where's the horse?"

You lead him to Funny Bits. Malford walks over to your horse and clips a long lead on her halter. He leads her into the shed and grooms the horse thoroughly. Then he saddles up and rides about the pasture. In a few moments he stops Funny Bits beside you and dismounts.

"Tremendous piece of horse flesh," he says. "She's already a winner. What type of competition did you have in mind?"

Choices: You decide to let Malford exhibit Funny Bits in the dressage classes (turn to page 74).
You want Malford to enter Funny Bits in the sulky races at the Bane County Fair (turn to page 76).

The lariat feels stiff and strange to you. You give a practice throw. The loop stays nice and round. It coils easy, but you immediately learn that you need gloves. The rope is rough and splintery.

You try again with gloves on. The first couple of throws never reach the fence posts. The rope's stiffness makes it more difficult to throw. You try harder until you finally hit the post.

With victory in sight you throw again. Bull's-eye! Your loop circles the post. You pull it tightly, knowing you have lassoed your first object. That evening you practice until you can rope a post ten feet away. Then you climb on Funny Bits and rope posts fifteen feet away. Your confidence grows. It shouldn't be too hard to rope a real calf.

But who has a calf to rope? Not you. That's for sure. So you begin on your little brother. He runs to mother, and you no longer can go that route. Soon the family dog and cat will no longer participate in your sport. Now you are in a dilemma.

One day as you are discussing the situation with a friend, he mentions an ad in the horse magazine. A roping club is meeting soon. "New members are invited to join," the ad says. You talk to your parents about it, and your mother gives you a letter from your uncle. He wants you to work on his ranch this summer.

Choices: **You decide to join the roping club (turn to page 78).**
You decide to work on your uncle's ranch (turn to page 109).

"You can just keep your dirty old nag," says one of the kids. "If I ever get a horse, it surely won't be an ugly one like that!"

"Right," says another. "I don't want to ride any old crate of bones either."

They leave. You stand combing your horse's hide with gentle, circular strokes that don't seem to do much. The hard rubber, serrated edges of the currycomb loosen the dandruff and it flakes out all over you and the horse. Removing the matted hair isn't easy either. The joy of ownership leaves. Why didn't you let the other kids stay and help?

You step back from the mare. She looks very tired but contented, almost asleep. Obviously you aren't hurting her but you know how you'd feel if someone had been pulling your hair. You reach for your dandy brush.

After a couple of swipes, the bristles are matted with loose hair and have lost most of their effectiveness. Maybe clippers would do the job better. But your clippers clog instantly.

Choices: **You are tired of working on your mare (turn to page 29).**
You decide to go back to using the currycomb (turn to page 30).

You stare defiantly at Malford. "I'm not your slave," you point out to him. "This is my mare. If you want anything else, you can get it yourself. I've done enough running. Now I want to watch as my foal is born."

Malford wipes his face. "Look, kid, I think this foal's going to be born breech. Instead of the nose coming out first, the foal's turned so the hind end will be first. You'd better get out of here if you can't cooperate." Malford yells for the owner who makes you leave the stable.

"Go to the lower stable and clean the stalls. I'll call you once the foal's born," the owner orders.

What an awful development this is! Your foal's in trouble, and you don't even know what's going on. Instead of watching the foal be born, you're stuck with the job you hate most. Angrily you shovel the manure into the wheelbarrow.

About an hour later, the owner rushes into the lower stable. "The colt's all right. You can come see him now," he yells excitedly.

You run all the way back to the main stable. A beautiful colt whose white rump is covered with black spots lies beside Funny Bits.

The owner points to one large spot on the colt's rump, which looks like a baby's outstretched hand. "That marks him as an exceptional animal. He will be sought after as a stud. You're a lucky kid."

You smile. You know that the colt and you will have lots of fun together in the years to come.

THE END

You and your friends make Indian headdresses by pasting colored chicken feathers to a headband. You wear squares of brown material over your jeans for breechclouts. You show your friends how to fringe the edges with scissors.

"Let's make a tepee," you suggest. "We'll cut down some tall, skinny trees from the woods behind Kevin's house, lace them together, and use some of Mom's old sheets to cover them."

Everyone helps you cut down five trees and trim off the branches. You drag them to your yard and lace them together with some branch stubs that hook the poles together in the right places. They form a five-legged tripod.

Your mother gives you a box of safety pins to hold the sheets together around the poles. But first you draw Indian pictures all over the sheets. When your wigwam is finished, you and your friends hold a council meeting inside.

Choices: **You cut down two more poles to make a travois (turn to page 85).**
You make Funny Bits into a war pony (turn to page 86).

The next Saturday night, you ask your parents if you can attend the early church service on Sunday morning. "The roping club has a special practice this Sunday," you lie. "May I go this once?"

Your parents agree, but just for today. Again, you bluff yourself into thinking that somehow everything will work out.

You ride Funny Bits to a deserted rodeo arena on the edge of town, three miles from your home. You're right on time for the 10:00 practice, but no one is there.

You practice your roping alone for what seems to be hours. Finally at 11:00 the leader and Chuck, the best roper of the club, show up. You practice with them, but time after time your rope misses the post. Your face gets redder each time.

"Aw, come on now," Chuck taunts, "nobody can be that bad!"

The next thing you know, Chuck complains to the leader, "This practice is boring. Let's try some real calf roping."

Now you feel really trapped. You're sure Chuck is trying to make you look even worse. After all, you can't rope a still object, much less a moving one.

Once the calf is in the arena, something unforeseen happens. Chuck is racing around after the calf, shouting "Yiiii!" at the top of his voice. Funny Bits is spooked by Chuck's screaming and the calf's resistant mooing. Your horse rears back. The next thing you know you're hitting the ground!

Turn to page 132.

Funny Bits stands quietly while you fashion ropes to look like a harness and hook her to the wagon. However, someone always has to lead her since she has never been taught to pull a cart. As the neighborhood kids see you and your friends riding in the wagon, they want to ride, too.

You hitch two wagons together and make a train. Soon you add another and another. The wagon train rumbles loudly down the sidewalk, but everyone in the neighborhood enjoys watching it.

Albert reads a notice in the newspaper of a coming parade. Everyone wants to enter Funny Bits and the neighborhood wagon train. You spend fifty cents on poster board to label the wagons.

You enter and win first prize for the most unusual entry. You all share the fifty dollars at the ice-cream store. Then you use the rest of the money to buy oats for Funny Bits. As she munches her treat, Funny Bits seems to smile and swishes her tail at **THE END.**

You wait until after supper to show your father your best papers from school. Then you lead him down to the workshop to show him the damaged bits.

He asks you to show him the travois poles, so you take him outside to view Albert's work.

"He does know what he's doing," your father finally admits. "But you disobeyed me. You will have to replace all of those drill bits."

You agree that is only fair, so you give him the money from your allowance cache in your room.

"It's time for you to learn how to use my tools," your father says with a grin. "If Albert's dad can teach him, I can surely teach you."

He spends an hour with you. The next day you make a planter box for your mother. You plan other projects for the future like a new barn for Funny Bits.

THE END

After dinner your father goes to his workshop to drill some holes in a piece of driftwood your mother wants to use as a candleholder. He finds the broken drill bits and calls you downstairs.

"You've not only broken my bits," he says, "you've also broken the rules. You will not get any allowance for a month."

"Do drill bits cost *that* much?" you ask.

"No, but you have also caused me an inconvenience."

You agree by nodding your head and start back up the stairs.

"Just a minute!" calls your father. "I'm not finished. You will also be grounded for two weeks for not telling me right away."

"But Elmer's birthday party is next week. I've already bought him a present."

Your father does not change his mind, so you are stuck with a game you already have. For the first time in your life you wish he had treated you like a little kid and just paddled **THE END.**

You take three handfuls of horsehair and begin to braid your horse's mane. The hair does not cooperate. It bunches wrong, slides out of the braid, and refuses to hold together. By the time your father returns, you are feeling very frustrated.

"This will never look right," you complain to him.

"Help me clean up this mess," your father says, "and I'll show you how my grandfather did it. He owned a horse farm in Kentucky, you know."

You help your dad rake the debris into a pile. Then he holds the garbage bag open while you stuff it with the old hair, burrs, and dirt. You are amazed at how neat a stall can look.

"Thanks, Dad," you say as you watch him twist the bag shut. He puts it by the door.

"Dip your comb into the water," he tells you, "and make the mane wet. It will braid easier that way." He takes the same hair and divides it into smaller parts. After he braids each section, he fastens it with a rubber band, and then does the tail. Funny Bits looks beautiful.

Choices: **You decide to enter her in the coming horse show (turn to page 59).**
You decide not to enter the horse show (turn to page 61).

When your father returns, you help him put the debris into the garbage bag.

"Dad," you say, "should I contact a vet and let Funny Bits have her foal here? Or would it be better to take her back to the stable?"

Your dad stands up, rubbing his neck with his left hand. "She's your horse. Remember your mom and I have left the choices up to you. If you want to see the foal born, she'll have to stay here. But the stable is also a wise choice."

He wires the garbage bag shut and takes it outside. You stand looking at your heavily laden mare. You want to do the very best for her.

Choices: **You take your mare back to Valley View Stables (turn to page 16).**
You decide to call a veterinarian to help when the time comes (turn to page 124).

You have just finished cleaning the stall area when your dad returns with the garbage bag.

"You are really growing up," he says, ruffling your hair fondly. "Help me put all of it in the bag, and I'll show you how to braid the mane and tail."

You grin and stuff the pile into the garbage bag as your father holds the bag open. He ties it closed and leaves it next to the door. Then he comes over to you.

"My grandfather showed me how to braid when I was a boy," he says. "Grandfather used to raise show horses in Kentucky, you know." You watch as he takes small amounts of hair and slowly begins to braid. "If this were for show, we'd add ribbons, but they're not really necessary. Hold this, while I find a rubber band." He fishes one out of a pocket and uses it to lock the braid.

You never dreamed Funny Bits could look so elegant. When you get to your room, you open up the current copy of *Horseman's Magazine* to the calendar listings of exhibitions and shows. One is being held in your hometown, and it's only a few weeks away. You are excited and scared at the same time since you've never shown a horse before.

Choices: **You enter the coming horse show (turn to page 59).**
You do not enter the horse show (turn to page 61).

You continue to groom your horse every day and rebraid the mane and tail until you know how to do it expertly. Funny Bits's hide has become shiny and clean from your excellent care.

You don't look so bad yourself. Your new jodh-purs, ratcatcher shirt, and jacket fit perfectly. You've shined your boots until they gleam. You set the small bowler hat squarely on your head and go out to saddle Funny Bits.

You sign up for the amateur saddle class. While you wait in line, Funny Bits prances and tosses her head quite often, but she is very well behaved. Other horses around you rear, jump at petty noises, and cause their riders to look bad.

You enter the ring gracefully. As you ride around the ring in pace with the others, the judge calls out commands: "Walk. Collected trot. Collected canter. Now reverse!" Your rhythm is perfect and Funny Bits's hooves strike the ground in a well-timed cadence. Around and around and around the ring once more. Finally it's over. The judge lines all the contestants up in front of the grandstand, and you realize that you are a winner.

Turn to page 60.

"Congratulations," he says handing you a second-place ribbon, "you are a good show-man." A photographer takes your picture as a journalist asks you questions. He tells you the picture and story will be in tomorrow's paper. You ride from the ring amidst the applause of your friends and family. When you dismount, you hook the ribbon to Funny Bits's bridle and whisper into the fuzzy ear, "Guess what! We know that this is not **THE END."**

"The stable owner wouldn't recognize her," you tell your dad.

He grins. "You're right. You've done a splendid job." He pets the mare on the neck and runs his hands down her sides. "We'll have to watch her closely so we don't lose her or your foal. Have you decided which veterinarian to call?"

You shake your head.

"I was wondering if we should take her back to the stable for the birthing," you say.

"That's a possibility," agrees your father, "but I think a local vet would be OK."

This is an important decision. Your father has told you stories about your grandfather's horse farm. Sometimes foals are lost at birth or the mother dies. You don't want that to happen to yours.

So you watch Funny Bits more closely every day. This makes you more fond of her. You are not sure when to summon the vet, and yet he has assured you that you are too worried. Funny Bits doesn't like the stable, but you could see her every night after school anyway. Finally you have to make the decision.

Choices: **You return your horse to the stable to have her colt (turn to page 16).**
You decide to let the colt be born at home (turn to page 124).
(turn to page 16). (turn to page 124).

Malford rushes out of the tack room and beats you to your mare's stall. You stand panting at the door, hoping to see the birthing process.

"Get a hot bran mash," Malford says. "After she gives birth, she'll need lots of vitamins."

You run down the stable aisle to the feed room. You mix three pounds of bran in a bucket with enough boiling water to moisten the mixture. You stir and salt it and then carry the bucket to Malford, running as fast as you can.

"Now," says Malford, as he puts the bucket aside, "get some clean towels, a pair of scissors, some tape, and a bottle of iodine."

You run to the tack room and search the shelves. When you find everything Malford wants you race back so you don't miss the foaling.

Malford looks up as you come in. "Put that stuff over against the wall. We'll need it later." He watches Funny Bits and ignores you.

Funny Bits swishes her tail and grunts.

"Go get a pail of warm water and some disinfectant," says Malford.

"What for?" you demand as you lean against the stall door panting. You want to stay and watch.

"Just get it and get it now!" he says. This order seems odd to you. Malford must be trying to get rid of you. After all, he hasn't used anything you've brought to him.

Choices: You go after the warm water and disinfectant (turn to page 98).

You refuse to do any more running (turn to page 48).

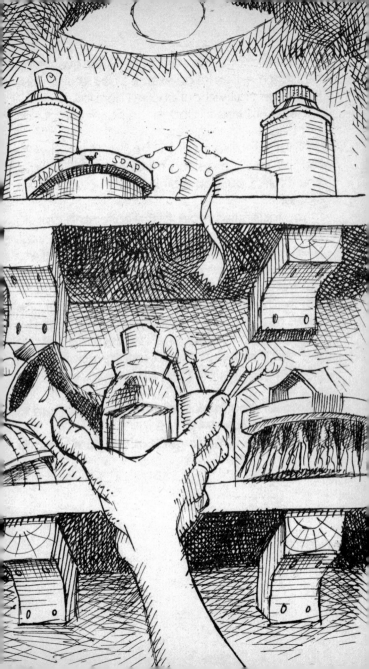

"That Malford!" you grumble. "After everything he's told me, he's let an exercise boy return Funny Bits to her stall without cooling her down."

Funny Bits tries to dodge the halter you put on her head.

"That exercise boy must have been awfully rough." You are getting madder by the minute. You think about complaining to the owner of the stable.

You fasten two ropes to the halter and crosstie Funny Bits by tying each rope to a different post. Then you get a bucket of cool water and begin to sponge bathe the mare. You try to towel her dry, but water seems to seep from her and her hide is getting hotter. The more you work with her, the more heat you feel coming through her skin. Her legs begin to tremble, and she tries to lie down in the stall. Immediately you unfasten both ropes and remove your bucket so she can rest.

Choices: **You think she will be all right (turn to page 94).**
You run to get Malford (turn to page 62).

You call the police first, and then your friend Alvin.

Soon after Alvin arrives, a squad car screeches to a halt in front of your house. You rush out to meet the detective.

"You say there's trouble at the Valley View Stables?" he asks. "Why didn't they call me?"

"The stable is a cover for horse thieves. They stole my horse."

"Calm down, now. Do you have proof of ownership?"

"Yes, come inside." You show him your receipt for Funny Bits and tell him your theory.

The detective walks to the squad car. "I will investigate this matter."

Choices: You and Alvin go with him (turn to page 96).

You let the officer investigate on his own (turn to page 97).

Immediately you and Alvin go over to Valley View Stables. You walk into the barn and go straight to Funny Bits's stall. It is empty. The floor has been freshly mucked out leaving a moist, wood bottom. There is no evidence that your horse was here. You turn around and find Malford watching you. He comes up and puts a warm arm about your shoulders.

"I'm sorry, kid," he says. "She was just so old she couldn't take it."

"Could I see her?" you ask. Tears are streaming down your cheeks, and you try to wipe them on your sleeve. Malford gives you a clean red handkerchief to wipe your face.

"Look, kid, I don't think it's good for anybody to mourn over the corpse of a horse. Why don't you go home and relax?" He gives you a kindly shove toward the entrance of the barn. "I'll take care of everything for you, OK?"

You turn around, and you give one last look at the stall door. Then you feel Malford's eyes burning into your head, so you turn and walk slowly down the aisle to the outside door.

Choices: You go back into the stable (turn to page 134).
You investigate the wagon in the stable yard (turn to page 127).

The kid screams as you grab his pony's bridle.

"Listen," you say, trying to reason with him again. "I've got to find Sissy's horse, and I can do it better and faster without you tagging after me. You're going back to Alvin."

He screams again and accidentally kicks his pony. The pony is already excited by the panic and whips his head around. He jumps and side-steps quickly, but you hang on while the brat continues to throw a tantrum on horseback.

"Find Sissy's horse," he screams louder and kicks the pony in the flanks again. The pony rears up and rips the reins out of your hands. Alvin's little brother gropes for something to hold onto, but loses his balance. He hits the ground with a thud. You grab the pony's bridle and check on the boy. He seems to be OK.

In fact, soon he is up and trying to get back in the saddle on the wrong side. You reach over and take him by the collar. He is so light that you actually lift him up and make him face you.

"Look. Neither of us can find Sissy's horse with you acting so awful. I'm going to take you home, if you don't straighten up. Understand?"

He nods. "Find Sissy's horse," he whispers.

You sigh and lift him back onto his pony.

Choices: **You give up and take Alvin's brother home (turn to page 128).**
You let him go with you to find the other horse (turn to page 110).

"Ride on ahead," you tell Alvin. "I'm going to cut across these cornfields and meet you at Duff's house." Alvin cannot bring his horse through the corn, but he will make good time following the road.

"OK," Alvin calls.

You barely hear him because you have leaped a fence and are racing down a row of corn. You wish that you had worn your track shoes instead of riding boots, but you think you're making better time than if you'd ridden Sissy's pony.

At the end of the cornfield, you follow a mere rut of a road that crosses a small bridge. Only one set of hoofprints are in the dust.

That must be Sissy on Funny Bits, you think. *Alvin's horse and the two ponies would look like a herd has passed.* You feel pretty good at being this far ahead of your friend. On the other side of the bridge, you climb a wooden fence and plunge into another cornfield. You know that you are getting very close to Duff's house as you trot down the straight rows of tasseling corn.

Choices: You sneak up on Alvin's sister to get Funny Bits back (turn to page 111). You walk up and demand your horse (turn to page 112).

You climb on her pony and find that it is as stubborn as Funny Bits is willing. Your legs are so long and the pony is so short that the toes of your boots drag in the dirt, making furrows deep enough to plant corn. You urge the pony over to the nearest tree and break off a huge branch.

With one stinging blow from the branch, the pony begins to buck beneath you. You try to lock your legs under his stomach to keep your seat, but that seems to make him madder. You soon find yourself leaning to one side. Immediately the pony rears, and you slide right off his back.

Choices: **You're quick enough to hang onto the pony's reins and continue to Duff's house (turn to page 28).**
The pony gets away from you, and you have to walk (turn to page 68).

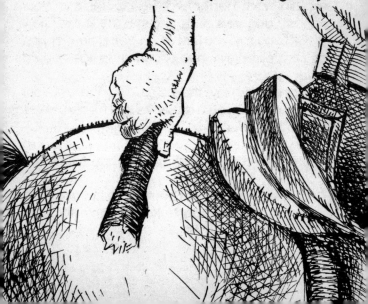

Funny Bits stands straight with an arched neck and flaring tail, and you bend over in the saddle to accept the ribbon for first place. Flash! A photographer takes your picture.

"Tell us how it feels to be a winner," shouts a reporter as he follows you from the winner's circle. You feel terrible because you know you didn't deserve to win. Instead you say it feels great. Everyone is congratulating you, but you just want to get far, far away.

The next morning you run to the drugstore to buy a newspaper. When you unfold it, you see the picture of you and Funny Bits jumping the brick wall. You look closely at the picture and see Funny Bits's left hind hoof hitting the top of the wall. Now it's obvious to everyone that you're not really the winner. You wish you had told the judge instead of hiding the truth. You decide to call the judge and explain what happened. He appreciates your honesty and says, "Next time let me know, OK?"

"OK," you say. You feel much better now, almost as if a great, ugly cloud of confusion has cleared away.

"By the way," says the judge, "I like the way your horse jumps. I need a horse like that for my stables. I'd like to buy him."

The offer stuns you. You know the judge would pay you a lot of money. Yet you love Funny Bits.

Choices: **You sell your horse (turn to page 101). You decide to keep Funny Bits (turn to page 44).**

"You're a fool!" exclaims the next contestant, but he smiles.

You watch his horse take the jumps easily. He's clear until the last when his horse clicks a rail just as Funny Bits did. You wait anxiously to hear his time. It is the same as yours. You are both tied for first place.

"We will have to have a runoff between contestants 28 and 46," the judge announces. "Will number 28 please reenter the ring."

"Ready?" asks the judge.

You nod affirmatively.

"Go!" His flag goes down, and you know the timer has begun. This time you are three-quarters of a second faster and have a perfect record.

Next, number 46 goes into the ring. He is fast, but he knocks down the last rail.

You win first prize and the ribbon for the Open Class.

Choices: You decide you've done enough for the day (turn to page 90).
You try for another ribbon by competing in the Amateur Class (turn to page 91).

Soon you are right behind the hunt master. You admire the smartness of his jodhpurs and red coat, and the way he controls his horse. You would like to lead a hunt someday yourself.

"Right dandy horse," he says, after he watches you handle a jump smoothly. "Should it be for sale, see me first."

You gasp. Sell Funny Bits? The thought had never entered your mind. When you are back at the farmhouse, the hunt master rides up to you.

"A right dandy hunt," he says, eyeing Funny Bits closely. "We couldn't have chosen a better day or a better route. The dogs caught the scent immediately and never lost it." He pauses in his reminiscing to stare straight at Funny Bits. "Right dandy horse," he says again. "I would like to make you an offer."

Choices: **You sell Funny Bits (turn to page 101).**
You enter Funny Bits in a jumping contest (turn to page 39).

Funny Bits tosses her head and walks sideways in her eagerness to be off. You hold her in with much effort until she can jump the first obstacle. Funny Bits goes over the fence with ease. However, the crowd ahead of you gets farther and farther away since your friend's pony is so slow. As the excitement disappears, Funny Bits quiets down, and you begin to enjoy the ride and the companionship of your friend.

"We're following a drag this year. Last year it took so long to find a fox that the hunt started late. Then they let the fox go."

"Do they always let it go?" you ask your friend.

"Not always, but foxes are getting scarce in this part of the country. If they're not around to kill some rabbits, the rabbits would take over." Your friend draws his mount up quickly as if shocked. "If rabbits multiplied, they'd eat more grass, and ..."

Funny Bits naturally stops to wait on your friend. As you look back, movement catches your eye. A red fox runs across the open area.

"Look!" you yell, pointing to the fox as it disappears into some brush nearby. "The hounds are coming!"

"Evidently that real fox has crossed the drag scent. What a hunt this is becoming!" He turns his pony around.

Choices: **You decide to follow the hounds (turn to page 72).**
You decide to stay with your friend on his slow pony (turn to page 107).

Malford begins showing you different training techniques. First he snaps a long lunge line to Funny Bits's bridle and makes her run around in large circles.

"This teaches horses how to relax and trust you," Malford says. He makes Funny Bits circle him at a walk, then a trot, and finally, a canter, until the horse is calm.

Then you watch Malford take Funny Bits over the cavalletti, which are long bars suspended by short X-shaped frames. They almost look like little jumps. After that comes the leg-yielding exercises. You think Funny Bits looks silly as she goes through the paces. Her hind feet don't follow her front feet as they would normally. Instead they're off to one side. Malford explains that "two tracking" teaches a horse to be sensitive to leg pressure.

Finally, after several weeks, Malford announces that Funny Bits is ready for the show ring.

On the day of the show, you proudly pin your owner's ribbon to your shirt. Funny Bits looks great. Her mane and tail are braided, her hooves shine, and the metal on the equipment gleams.

The loudspeaker announces your horse's number. Malford enters on Funny Bits at a collected canter. They stop. Malford salutes the judge and starts a series of intricate movements. Funny Bits crisscrosses the ring at a trot, canters in place, and turns on her haunches perfectly.

When the judge calls out the winner, you and Malford proudly accept the trophy. This is definitely not **THE END.**

"You can beat him, Funny Bits. I don't have any doubts," you say as you run your hand down her strong neck. You check her girth, give her a sip of water, and pick her hooves. You're a bit nervous so you pray for a clear head. If Devil Boy's owner wins the jumping class, he'll never let you live it down.

The loudspeaker announces the class. You're the first to go. You and Funny Bits give it everything. Funny Bits turns, jumps, crosses the course, jumps, does a figure eight, flies over the brick wall, and finally crosses the timing line.

"One point five six," says the timekeeper. You groan. It's a fast time for this course, but it may not give you the edge you need to beat number 46.

The next competitor is 46. Devil Boy looks eager and rested. He leaps the first fence at a full gallop. Number 46 reins him around into position for the second jump along the rail of the ring. You can see his determination. Devil Boy races for the next fence, looses his rhythm, and, just when you think he'll balk before the gate, springs almost straight up and clears the fence. The crowd is roaring. Devil Boy loops around at full speed and recklessly heads for the coop.

They clear the coop by feet. The rider pulls out his crop and heads for the post-and-rail jump. A split second before they get to the jump, Devil Boy puts his head down, locks his hind legs, and swerves out of the jump. The rider flips over Devil Boy's shoulder and misses the post of the jump by inches. He's OK, but his bragging days have come to **THE END.**

A few days later, Malford takes you and Funny Bits out to Valley View Stables to rent a sulky racing cart. It's a seat on a light aluminum frame, supported by two bicyclelike tires. You pull at one of the long poles on the front and find it is easily moved.

"You'll soon make enough prize money to buy your own cart," he says optimistically.

You're not so sure. "Malford, I've been reading about trotters and I've found they're a special breed called standardbreds. They aren't regular riding horses; they're trained to trot only. I'll miss riding. Funny Bits is more than just a trotter."

"You better believe it," says Malford lightly. "Funny Bits is the best. You just watch. She's going to win every time."

Choices: You race in the Bane County Fair (turn to page 126).
You change your mind and decide to retire Funny Bits (turn to page 44).

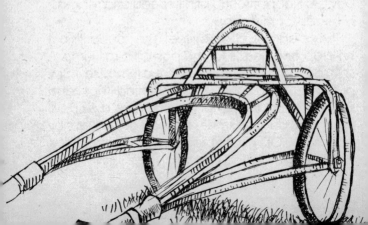

You and your friend search and search for a bola and cannot find one in the stores.

"It's a weapon consisting of two or more stone or iron balls attached to the ends of a cord. You hurl it at an animal to entangle it," you explain. when the clerk doesn't know what a bola is.

"I saw cowboys break a cow's legs with one on tv," your friend says.

The clerk looks frightened. "It sounds like it's too dangerous for kids your age. Why don't you buy some marbles and play a safe game like that?"

"No, thanks," you tell the man. You leave the store feeling very sad. You have tried everywhere to buy a bola.

"Maybe we don't have the right name for it."

"I know. Let's go to the library and see if we can find out some more about them," you suggest.

Choices: **You go to the library (turn to page 122).**
You decide to give up and look at saddles instead (turn to page 136).

You go to the first roping club meeting. Several other boys and girls are there, too. The leader introduces everyone, and then he takes all the members out to his backyard to rope fence posts.

"That was a stingy throw," he says to you, after you have missed the post for the twentieth time. "Give yourself more rope and throw harder."

He takes your rope and shows you exactly what he means.

"Now you try it."

You miss on the next attempt, and he shows you again. On your fifth try the rope circles the post.

"I did it!" you yell to everybody. They enjoy your success. Now you know that you can become a first-class roper.

As the meeting closes, the leader gives you a printed list of membership requirements.

1. Dues—$15 a month.
2. Every member must attend the Sunday practice from 10 A.M. to noon.
3. All members must participate in three rodeos a year.

Three rodeos! How exciting! And the fifteen dollars your grandmother gave you for your birthday will pay the dues for the first month. But 10:00 A.M. on Sunday? You know your parents will not want you to miss Sunday school and church.

Choices: You join the club (turn to page 51).
You decide to try out for the musical at church instead (turn to page 26).

Your father enters the room.

"How does one figure a tithe?" you ask, showing him your money.

He sits down beside you. "To find the amount of your tithe, you simply divide the total by ten."

You continue to look puzzled.

He grins. "It's not all that hard. Look. If you had a dollar," he writes $1.00 on a piece of scrap paper so that you can easily see it, "you can divide by ten by moving the decimal point one place to the left." He puts a decimal point before the number one and makes a curvy arrow to show the original decimal point moved: $.100. "Now it reads .10. Ten is one-tenth of one hundred. Here you try it with $3.60."

You write $3.60 on the paper and then put a decimal point in front of the three.

"It's 36¢," you say proudly.

"Right. Now figure your own tithe, and put it into a special envelope for God."

When you are done, he pats your shoulder. "That is your tithe. If you give more, it would be an offering."

Choices: **You decide to earn more money before going to the tack store to buy your saddle (turn to page 80).**
You decide to spend your money now (turn to page 136).

When you take your tithe to Sunday school, you try to slide your bulky envelope into the class offering plate. Clunk! The sound of metal hitting metal breaks the silence.

"Where'd you get all that money?" several kids ask.

You explain your business and how profitable it's been.

"But why are you giving it all to the church?" they want to know.

"I'm not giving all," you say, "this is only a tithe."

With the help of your teacher you explain tithing.

The next evening several members of the class come over to ride Funny Bits. "We want to help you make more money to tithe," they say. You gladly accept their money and give them rides. After that they come quite often, and you soon are able to tithe and still buy that new saddle.

Soon the other kids begin to follow your example and tithe, too. One Sunday morning your teacher has an idea. "I think our class could support Gene Thomas, a missionary for our church in South America. Would everyone like to do that?"

You all agree it would be fun to contribute to this ministry.

About a month later Gene Thomas sends the class a cassette tape and some pictures of his work with young people in Argentina. He has started a group that sings for churches and tells people how God is working in their lives.

On Gene's next furlough, he comes to your class. The other kids tell how you started them tithing. Gene smiles at you and gives you his *vaquero* hat—a real cowboy hat from Argentina.

You put it on proudly. You are determined that your support for him will never come to **THE END.**

You whistle happily as you ride Funny Bits down the street to the tack store. Her ears wiggle back and forth as she listens. Tying her reins to the hitching post, you walk straight inside to the counter and lay all your money down in front of the clerk.

You point to the leather saddle you have admired in the shop window. "I want to buy that saddle," you tell him. Quickly he counts your money.

"I'm sorry," he says turning to you, "but the price just went up yesterday. It will cost you twenty dollars more."

"But I don't have twenty more dollars." Within seconds your dream has vanished!

"I can sell you a secondhand saddle," the clerk says, walking over to another one. You touch it. It's a leather saddle, but it's a little worn and not very fancy.

You walk over to the window and look out at Funny Bits. What would she suggest if she could talk? After all she helped earn the money and the saddle is for her.

Choices: **You buy the secondhand saddle (turn to page 92).**
You decide not to buy anything today (turn to page 93).

You get the drill for Albert, knowing that you are breaking a definite rule. Since your father is at work, you cannot ask him now.

"I'll need an extension cord and some other bits," Albert tells you. He seems so confident that you feel better. Everything will be all right. You return from your dad's workbench with his neatly coiled, orange extension cord and a kit of drill bits.

Albert fits a drill bit into the mouth of the drill while you uncoil the extension cord and plug it into an outside socket. Albert attaches the drill to the cord and tries out the drill. It buzzes beautifully. But when he tries to drill into the hard wood he breaks the bit within seconds. He tries another and breaks it, too.

"I need a larger bit," he says, putting in the largest one. He drills all the holes you need, and helps you put the tools away. As you come out of the workshop, you notice that your dad has just come home.

Choices: You tell your dad you borrowed the tools (turn to page 53).

You do not say anything (turn to page 54).

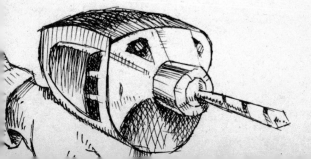

Marie soon tires of holding the poles, and they slip from her grasp.

"I give up," she says. "Let's play something else."

"Just one more try," you plead.

"If you can't do a thing right, there's no use trying," Albert mutters as he begins to walk away.

Choices: You give in and let Albert use the drill (turn to page 83).

You give up the idea completely (turn to page 87).

The travois pictured in your history book at school has two poles that are joined together by a platform. You find a large piece of canvas and attach it to the poles. Then you saddle Funny Bits and put the poles through the stirrups. You tie a piece of rope to each pole and fasten the ropes to the saddle horn.

"I get to ride first," demands Marie. Before you can stop her, she plops down on the travois and the poles slide out.

You try the travois without anyone or anything on it, and the primitive vehicle works. Still you built it to ride on, not just for Funny Bits to pull.

"Why don't you let me ride Funny Bits and hold the poles?" Marie suggests.

"It would be smarter to use your dad's drill to make holes in the poles. Then the ropes can't slip out," Albert suggests.

Your dad isn't home, but you know he doesn't allow you to use his tools, especially the electric ones.

When you explain this to Albert, he objects. "My dad taught me to use a drill. I can drill the holes. Your dad will never know the difference."

Choices: **You use the drill (turn to page 83).**
You let Marie hold onto the poles while riding (turn to page 84).

Funny Bits lets you and your friends ride bare-back. Your horse doesn't seem to mind your slid-ing all over her or crawling between her legs or trying to ride Apache, which is hanging onto one side to hide from the enemy on the other.

But soon Funny Bits tires of the game. She keeps trying to eat grass or head for the grain bin.

"She's a lazy old nag," complains one friend.

"You're right," says another.

"I'm going to go play ball," says a third. "Any-body want to go and play with me?"

Even you are tired of Funny Bits. You put her back in the shed, and follow your friends to the ball park.

That evening when you are lying in bed thinking about the day, you admit to yourself that you had a lot more fun playing ball than making an unwill-ing horse into a war pony. But tomorrow is another day. Your patience has not yet reached **THE END.**

"Hey, you guys," you holler. "There's going to be a special missionary speaker at our church tonight. How about coming with me?"

"Church?" scoffs Albert. "That sounds stuffy."

"Not missionary services," you explain. "Missionaries tell great adventure stories, and allow kids to handle all kinds of different things from another country. Sometimes they teach us how to sing a song in a foreign language."

"I'll ask my mom," says Marie. "Maybe she'll let me come."

Albert hangs around after the others leave.

"You don't really want to go to that old church service," he says. "Come with me, and we'll see *The Rustlers* at the movie theater."

**Choices: You go to the show (turn to page 4).
You go to the missionary service (turn to page 88).**

Marie comes running into your yard. "Hey! My mom says I can go. Is it all right if my brother Jimmy comes, too?"

"Sure," you say. By the time service starts, you have seven friends sitting beside you in the missionary service. Your pastor says the missionary is from Africa when he introduces him.

"I have a surprise to give to the person who brought the most guests to this meeting tonight," begins the missionary.

You quickly count your friends again.

"Is there anyone who brought ten?"

Your heart sinks, but as no one responds, you realize you still have a chance.

"Did anyone bring five?"

You jump to your feet. "I have seven friends."

"Would they stand up?"

They stand beside you, and the man gives each of you a tiny gazelle carved out of wood.

During the service the offering plate is passed. You and your friends have forgotten to bring any money along. At the end of the service, the missionary holds up a large poster listing several needs on the field. You wish you could do something to help him.

Choices: You decide to start a group project to supply one of the needs (turn to page 120).
You decide to pray about it (turn to page 121).

Your second day is harder than the first. When you try to get out of bed, every muscle protests. There is so much pain in your legs and arms that you can hardly walk. Right after breakfast you have to saddle a horse. You are slow because your muscles hurt each time you move.

"Hustle it," commands Dave. "We've got work to finish."

"I can't," you moan, but he laughs. This makes you so mad you scramble up into the saddle. The saddle hurts your tailbone and rubs the insides of your legs. But Dave shows you no mercy.

"Ride 'em, cowboy!" he yells when two calves are running away from the herd. They escape him and he yells at you again. "Go get them. I've got to keep the rest of the herd intact."

You and Funny Bits follow the calves through the fence. Your horse seems instinctively to know your mission. Funny Bits gallops after the calves as they twist and turn in the brush. Finally she circles them and brings them to the fence. The calves turn back. Funny Bits halts on her back legs and swings around so fast that you slide off. Your bottom lands in a patch of prickly pear cactus. You decide that your days as a ranch hand have come to **THE END.**

As you ride out of the ring, a man calls your name and comes toward you. You dismount to talk to him.

"That was an excellent ride," he says. "That's a great horse! I would like to buy her if you would sell her."

You stand in momentary shock. Funny Bits isn't for sale. How could the man have gotten that idea?

"I do a lot of riding," he continues, "and one of my horses is getting quite elderly. I have been looking for a special horse to take its place. Your horse would be perfect."

Then you realize that Funny Bits is the winner of the jumper's class, and therefore quite a valuable animal. She turns her soft nose around to nuzzle your shoulder. She is not only your horse, but she has also become your friend.

"I'll give you any reasonable price," the man insists.

Still you hesitate. Funny Bits is quite valuable, and you have the chance to make a lot of money.

Choices: You sell Funny Bits (turn to page 101).
You keep her (turn to page 22).

Competitor number 46 is also in the Amateur Owner jumping class. He comes up to you before the event begins.

"I bet you that my horse is better than yours."

"What?" you are shocked. You look at him and then his horse.

"My horse Devil Boy is a better horse than your nag. He'll beat yours easily this time."

You do not believe him. "Why your horse is tired after the last class. Funny Bits is still fresh. You're crazy if you think you'll win."

He becomes angry. "That's not so. You're afraid to bet, because you know Devil Boy is the better mount."

Despite his ridicule, you shake your head no!

The evil-looking man hesitates, but then moves on. You can see him suggesting the same thing to another competitor.

Turn to page 75.

You bring the saddle out of the shop and swing it up onto Funny Bits's back. Clumsily you cinch it, and then pull yourself up into the saddle. The leather feels slick and cool compared to the sweaty horse's back. But the stirrups are too long.

The clerk has been watching out the window. Now he comes out of the store. "I'll shorten those stirrups for you," he offers, "if you'll hold your horse still."

"Sure," you say. "Thanks a lot!"

Soon you and Funny Bits are headed for home. But when you take the saddle off the horse, you notice it needs some special soap. The sweat from Funny Bits's back is turning the leather dark. You ride Funny Bits back to the store.

"Do you have any saddle soap?" you ask the clerk. He gets it for you; the soap costs every penny you have left.

When you get home, you are too tired to clean the saddle and polish it. But the next evening, you set it on a sawhorse in your father's workshop and begin to rub the soap on the leather with an old, soft cloth. Soon your shoulder muscles begin to scream from the exertion. Now you know what real work is. Caring for a horse and keeping the riding equipment in order seem never to come to **THE END.**

Your mother does not seem to be surprised that you did not buy a new saddle.

"There's always another day," she says. "No matter, dear. You just have time to get cleaned up for Wednesday night service."

"Do I have to go?"

She gives you that special look that says you have no choice. You get cleaned up in time, but decide to sit sullenly on the back pew. Usually your friends sit back there with you and you have a pretty good time. Tonight none of them come. You sit alone. The preacher speaks, and you become convicted for not tithing. You are very, very miserable.

Choices: **You ask God to forgive you and decide to tithe (turn to page 80).**
You decide to forget this meeting as soon as possible (turn to page 129).

Your frustration cools as you make the homeward trip. By the time you get there, you're back to normal and whistling. Nobody's home so you raid the icebox and find some pizza left over from another meal. You cook it in the microwave, pour a glass of milk, and prepare to watch some tv.

For once no one's home to make you change channels or lower the volume. The tube flickers on. You sip your milk. Then you take a bite of pizza. You brush the crumbs from your lap, and become involved in the program.

The phone rings.

You let it ring.

It continues to ring until you cannot ignore it any longer. You get up and answer it.

"This is the owner of the Valley View Stables. Your mare, Funny Bits, is foaling."

"Oh."

Suddenly you know why she was so sweaty.

You jump on your bike and head for the stable to get Malford.

Turn to page 62.

The other kids take the field while you step up to the plate. The pitcher tosses a high-arching, underhand pitch to you. You swing! The ball flies past you and into the catcher's mitt. Strike one!

This time the pitch is almost flat—just the way you like it. You swing and spin around in disbelief: you've missed again. Now you're mad.

The next pitch arches gracefully toward you. You watch it come in and swing.

Strike three!

You stomp out of the batter's box and grab your mitt. You've had enough of this foolishness, you think to yourself. Who needs softball? Your softball days and your friendships are about to come to **THE END.**

You and the officer arrive at Valley View Stables just as a wagon with a dead horse is pulled out. The officer takes you straight to the owner of the stable even though you want to see the carcass on the wagon.

"I'd like to see this young man's horse, Funny Bits," the officer says to the owner.

"That horse died in foaling. You will not find her in her stall. She's already on the wagon outside to be carted to the refinery."

You do not believe him. You and the police officer go to the stall where you last saw your horse. It is empty. Even the straw has been mucked out. You turn and go out to the wagon where the dead horse lies.

Choices: You recognize the horse as yours (turn to page 127).
You do not recognize the horse (turn to page 133).

You go back inside your house, but you cannot sit still. Is Funny Bits really dead? Finally you cannot stay home another minute.

As you head for the Valley View Stables, your mind reflects the scenes in the movie. Beautiful colts and their dams removed from the stables to be replaced with cold, lifeless bodies.

You see Funny Bits as you saw her last. Her red face lifted, the fuzzy ears pricked forward to welcome you with a nicker.

When you enter the parking lot of Valley View Stables, you see the policeman talking to the owner. Then you see a flat wagon, hooked to a small tractor, waiting in the middle of the yard. You rush over to it. A dead horse is lying there.

Choices: You recognize the horse as yours
(turn to page 127).
It's not Funny Bits **(turn to page 133).**

You run back with the warm water and sponge as quickly as you possibly can. A wet mass lies on the straw floor in front of Malford. You quietly walk toward him, carrying the hot water and sponge. The atmosphere is one of awe and wonder.

Malford doesn't look up or thank you. He whispers, "I need more towels from the tack room."

You linger around so you can look closer.

"Get me some clean towels," he says sternly.

His tone makes you turn quickly and run down the stable aisle. What does he want more towels for? Why is he so grouchy? Who does he think he is anyway? It's your foal.

When you get back to the stall, you give the towels to a grinning Malford. Funny Bits is standing over a wet heap, nosing it.

"It's a colt," he says taking the towel from you. "A right pert little feller, too." He sponges the colt with the warm water, and you see him dry its hide gently.

The foal stands. He is a light gray with black spots all over him.

"He's a leopard Appaloosa," Malford says, "and a right nice one at that." He grins. "I'll buy him from you, kid."

His face has become serious. You understand that his words were not spoken in jest.

Choices: You sell the colt to Malford (turn to page 131).
You decide to keep the colt (turn to page 14).

You swing. The ball is in the catcher's glove.

"Strike three," he says. "You're out!"

The team groans, but Alvin as captain comes to the rescue by hitting a home run. Consequently your team wins by one point. Maybe it does pay to "Do unto others as you would have them do unto you."

Everyone is ecstatic. They decide to follow you home. You find Funny Bits fully rested from the morning exercise so you saddle up.

"Funny Bits will have a foal in a couple months, so only one can ride at the most."

"Let Alvin ride. He's the captain," the boys decide.

Alvin rides as you lead Funny Bits to the nearest ice-cream parlor.

"Hey!" says Todd to get everyone's attention. "Let's make Funny Bits our mascot. Then we'll be the only team in town with a horse as a mascot."

The vote is unanimous. Funny Bits has become the official mascot for the team.

Alvin looks at you and says, "Would you rather be our team manager and keep score?"

The question surprises you until you realize he is suggesting a way for you to stay with the team and not have to be embarrassed because you are a poor ball player.

"Sure," you say. Relief floods over you. Your ball-game days will be much more enjoyable in the future.

THE END

The man pays a good price for Funny Bits. You give your horse one last pat as you accept the check and walk away. It seems strange to be walking after you've ridden so much.

"Hey! Would you like a ride?"

You turn. A friend of yours rides up behind you on his pony.

"Where?" You kid him. "On the tail?"

"No, behind me. There's plenty of room."

You crawl on his horse behind him and ride double.

"Will you buy another horse?" he asks.

"Maybe."

"Don't you *want* another horse?" he asks. He is surprised you sold Funny Bits.

"Well, I don't know," you hedge. Now that you've owned a horse you realize what a lot of work and responsibility it is.

"You've got en___ money to get a really good mount." ___ friend is testing your attitude. "I have a ___ that has a sorrel for sale ..."

You decide to buy another horse (turn to page 105).

You're still not sure (turn to page 106).

102

You let each one crawl onto Funny Bits and take
a turn riding at a walk around the block. The rider
always sits tall in the saddle. He waves to each
one on the ground as if he were Roy Rogers.
Funny Bits obliges each with a great ride. Then you
unsaddle and put Funny Bits back into the shed.

Everyone hangs around not knowing what to
do next.

"Let's go play ball," someone suggests.

"Would you like to play ball?" asks Alvin.

"Sure," you say with everyone else. "Just let me
get my glove."

"You can be the first to bat," everyone says.

"We'll make you the team's captain," says Alvin.
Quickly the others agree. You know that they are
honoring you, because you let them ride Funny
Bits. It makes you feel good, but you know that
Alvin has always been the team captain and first
at bat. He is the best ball player in the neighborhood, and you've always been the worst.

Choices: You become captain and bat first
(turn to page 95).
You decide to bat first, but allow your
friend Alvin to be the team captain
(turn to page 99).

You canvass the entire neighborhood. "I'd like you to have my calling card," you say when someone answers the door, "so you can contact me if you need help. I run errands for a quarter."

A couple of the older people have letters to mail. Another neighbor needs something from the K Mart. A few mothers with young children ask you to get groceries for them. That evening you are so tired you fall asleep watching your favorite tv show.

Your mother taps you on the shoulder. "Telephone."

What next? you wonder as you walk to the phone and take the receiver.

"My kitty has been frightened into a tree," says an elderly woman's voice. "Would you come and get her down?"

Choices: You rescue the cat (turn to page 114). You turn the errand down (turn to page 118).

When you get home from school Thursday evening, your mother gives you a list of twenty-three phone numbers.

"These people have errands for you to run in response to your advertisement in the paper."

After telephoning the tenth number, you groan as you hang up the receiver. Automatically you reach for the list and begin dialing the next number. You had no idea that there would be such a demand for your services.

As you talk with the next one you add her address and desire to the list. When you have called all twenty-three, you look at the notes you've made and find you can group the errands together according to the addresses. You decide to start with those closest to home.

"Bye, Mom," you say as you leave. You feel just like your father when he says, "I don't know when I'll be home."

You deliver mail, buy groceries, and wrap gifts. It's almost dark when you finally go home. Sitting in your favorite chair, you fall asleep before you can turn the tv on with the remote control. Your mother taps you on the shoulder and points at the telephone.

With misgiving you answer it. An elderly lady says her cat is up a tree and she can't get it down.

Choices: You rescue the cat (turn to page 114).
You decline the job (turn to page 118).

You go back to Valley View Stables to look for another horse.

"The Appaloosa mare and the pinto pony are still for sale," says the owner.

"Can I see them again?"

"Sure." He shows you the Appaloosa first. The mare has gained some weight. Her ribs aren't as prominent. She's looking much better, with a shiny hide and a tangle-free mane and tail.

"She'll foal any day now," the owner says. "Last time you were here I wouldn't have thought she would make it, but now I'm pretty certain."

You nod. "Where's the pinto?"

"Over here."

The little pinto comes right up to you and nuzzles your fingers. Her warm brown eyes plead for you to give her a real home.

Choices: You buy the Appaloosa (turn to page 16).

You buy the pinto (turn to page 7).

You mope about the house for about a week trying to find something exciting to do. Finally you call Valley View Stables.

"I'd like to buy another horse," you tell the owner as you give him your name. "Is the pinto or the Appaloosa mare still for sale?"

"No, but I have a chestnut quarter horse."

"Chestnut? What kind of a horse is that? I thought a chestnut was a tree!"

He laughs. "Chestnut is a color. A chestnut horse is reddish brown with a cream-colored mane and tail."

"Like a palomino?" You become excited.

"Darker."

"I'll be over in a little bit."

The chestnut isn't as beautiful as Funny Bits, but she is gentle. You fall in love with her, and buy her. As you are taking her home, you wonder what you are going to name her.

Why not call her Funny Bits, too, just like the other horse? You like the idea so much that you do it.

When you get home, your mother reminds you of the missionary service.

"Do I have to go?" you ask.

"I thought you wanted to go," she replies.

Choices: You decide to do something new and different (turn to page 24).
You decide to invite all your friends to the missionary service (turn to page 87).

Your friend grins as he sees the horses of the other riders behind the hunt master.

"We'll not have trouble keeping up with them now. Their mounts are tired while ours are still quite fresh."

The hunt master blows a horn as he races across the field behind the hounds. You follow beside your friend as the best riders charge past to catch up with the hunt master. Still you and your friend are able to stay close to the front. The baying of the hounds seems to be more excited and the volume rises.

Turn to page 108.

"I think they've treed the fox. Let's hurry so we can see them catch it. I didn't get to see that part last year."

"Will they let it go again?" you ask.

"I think so, but let's hurry!"

Both of you kick the sides of your horses to spur them on. You arrive just as the hunt master collars his hounds and rewards them with fresh liver for treeing the fox. Everyone agrees to let the fox have his freedom.

"I'm coming to the next hunt, too," your friend says as you meander home.

"So am I," you comment. "I'm sorry that this hunt has come to **THE END.**"

"Let's see how well you can ride and rope," your uncle says after you arrive. He watches you saddle Funny Bits and mount. "I'll open the gate to that pasture. You bring me one of those calves."

You ride out confidently and circle the herd. You see a small red calf with a white face who looks easy to handle. You gallop towards him and the herd splits.

You follow the stampeding calf, but he outruns your pony. Immediately you see a slower animal and decide to rope it. Your fifth loop misses again. Your uncle calls you back.

"That's enough. I want you to ride out with Cowboy Dave to fix fences."

Cowboy Dave calls it riding fences. You call it boring. Every time you find the barb wire has broken or a post is down, you and Dave repair it. At the end of the day you are exhausted.

Dave shakes your hand. "You'll do," he says. "See you tomorrow, and we'll ride the south fence."

You unsaddle and walk stiffly to the house.

Choices: You decide to try working with Dave another day (turn to page 89).

You decide to ask your uncle for a different job (turn to page 137).

"All right," you say to Alvin's little brother. "Now we've got to retrace our steps and find Sissy's horse. I'm going to let you have the reins back." You stop when you see a mischievous grin on his face and a defiant glint come into his eyes.

"OK, I'll just keep the reins." You climb on and start off leading little brother's horse.

"No! I'll be good," he yells.

After this you have no more trouble with little brother. You soon learn that he can spot horse tracks easily. He becomes a valuable asset to you, and you progress quite rapidly. Suddenly you come to a familiar area.

Turn to page 128.

Hidden within the corn rows, you begin to feel like a master spy. Alvin's sister will probably have tied Funny Bits to the hitching post in the shade of the old cottonwood next to Duff's back door. Her next move will be to find Duff himself.

So you sneak around to the tree. Funny Bits isn't tied to the post. You are momentarily distressed until you realize you have beaten her and Funny Bits to Duff's. A good feeling runs through your veins.

You decide to hide in the cornfield until you see Sissy ride Funny Bits into the yard and up to the tree. Sure enough, within seconds she's there. She slides off like a pro and flips the reins over the post. Without a second glance, she walks through Duff's back door.

Scrambling from the field, you charge toward Funny Bits. Just as you reach your horse to claim the reins, Duff and the girl come out of the house. Maybe now you can learn about polo.

Turn to page 28.

You come out of the cornfield and walk right up to Duff's back porch. You knock on the door loudly. He answers, but before you can talk, a shout turns you around. Alvin's sister enters the yard on Funny Bits.

She rides up to you as if she had expected to see you here, slides off, and hands over the reins. "You have a nice horse," she says. "I'll trade mine for yours any day."

"She sure looks like a winner," Duff agrees. "Tie her up under the tree, and come in to chat for a while. Where's Alvin and the little boy?"

"They're coming," Sissy replies.

You stare at her. She is so composed for a horse thief.

Turn to page 28.

"I'll be your first customer," says your mother, handing you a grocery list and a couple of dollars. "I want you to get me a dozen eggs, a gallon of milk, and a pound of cream cheese."

"OK!" you yell and run out the door. You mount Funny Bits and gallop the two blocks to the store. Quickly you get the groceries and come back at a slower pace.

"Thanks, darling," your mother says when you set the sack on the counter. "I had to make a cake for supper tonight."

You decide to get a drink of water. Soon she comes over to show you three broken eggs.

"This is OK for me, because I'm going to use them in my cake, but you are going to have to be more careful with your customers' groceries," she says. "Oh, I haven't paid you yet. Take a quarter from the change you brought back."

You pick up a quarter and put it in your pocket. The errand business seems to be more work than pay.

Choices: You offer pony rides instead (turn to page 22).
You reorganize your errand business (turn to page 119).

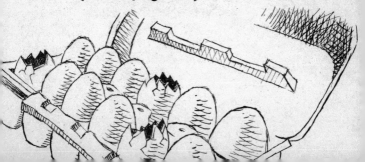

You bicycle to the woman's house and find the cat perched on a maple limb ten feet in the air.

"May I borrow a ladder?" you ask.

"Sure. There's one in the garage."

You climb up the ladder until you are eyeball-to-eyeball with the cat. You reach out to get it, and the cat climbs upward. You climb up another step. You still cannot touch it. Gingerly you look at the ground and climb the last two steps. You stroke the cat's head, and it begins to purr. But it will only allow you to touch its head. Soon you lose patience and grab the cat by the head.

"MEOW!"

You should be the one screaming, you think. Here you are teetering on the top of the ladder, trying to hold onto a screeching cat whose claws would make a mechanical knife look harmless. You cram the animal into the large pocket on your coat and crawl slowly down the ladder. At the bottom you let the owner pull her cat out. Thank goodness, it did not smother.

Pocketing a quarter, you wonder what will be next. But you're happy because the lady is happy, and the cat didn't manage to mangle you with its evil claws. You whistle as you ride home. This episode has happily come to **THE END.**

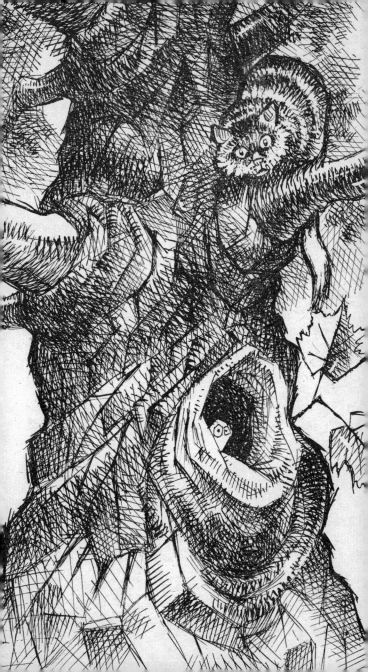

You become a popular baby-sitter because you let the kids ride Funny Bits and often take them to the park. At first mothers are afraid the horse might hurt their children, but eventually they realize how gentle Funny Bits is. They soon recommend you to their friends: "My children are usually worn out from a day with Funny Bits. I can usually give them a bite of supper and send them straight to bed. Such bliss."

"Better than any television," grunts a grouchy one.

You grin anyway. Taking advantage of this advertising, you teach the kids how to groom Funny Bits and muck out the stalls. As long as you supervise, you have a grand labor force. Their reward is an extra ride on Funny Bits. You hope this setup will never come to **THE END.**

You put your left foot in the stirrup and swing your right leg up over the horse. Suddenly you feel like royalty as you sit there in the saddle looking down at your friends.

"See you later," you say. "Giddap, Funny Bits." You ride your horse down to the park and over to the lake. As you ride, you occasionally think of your friends waiting for you to come back.

"Ah, let them wait," you mutter as you turn Funny Bits onto a well-marked path. "If they want to ride a horse so badly, they can rent one from the town stables or get one of their own."

It is a lonely path, but you and Funny Bits follow it. Leafy branches form an arch over the path, and the breeze is cool. You watch the flight of several birds from tree to tree. Squirrels chatter at you from the tops of the pines. Your ride takes most of the day. You arrive home very hungry. None of your friends are around.

You phone your best friend. His mother answers. "Alvin's down at the ball diamond," she says.

"Thank you," you tell her and hang up. You go down to the diamond and find the whole gang playing. They ignore you. Finally you walk up to Alvin.

"Can I play?"

"No, all the positions are filled."

You watch them for a few moments and then walk home. Your friendship has come to **THE END.**

You continue to turn down jobs that seem to be too much work. Soon the phone calls become less frequent. Two weeks later, there are absolutely no calls for you.

"What's wrong with people?" you ask. "For about ten days they about drove me nutty wanting errands run. I was to go all over creation trying to satisfy their latest whims. Now they don't even bother to call."

"I think they'd rather do it themselves than listen to your sad story or watch you do it sloppily," your mother remarks.

"I did my best!" you exclaim. You cannot stare her down. "Oh, well, if anyone calls, tell them I'm too busy."

You walk into the living room and flip on the tv. It's a lousy show, the most boring one of the season, and you've seen it about three times. You watch it anyway since there's nothing else to do. Your business has abruptly come to **THE END.**

You decide to use your bicycle for most errands, your wagon for large grocery orders, and Funny Bits for fast deliveries and messages. In the basement you paint a sign to advertise your business:

ERRANDS
25¢ for short trips
More for longer ones
Call 872-6543

Mom and Dad allow you to nail it to the front fence. You're sure it will be good advertising. And what about a newspaper ad?

Choices: **You have 500 calling cards printed (turn to page 103).**
You put an ad in the local paper (turn to page 104).

All the kids meet in Funny Bits's shed after school. You place bales of straw around for chairs.

"How are we going to make money? Everything on that list takes money," you say.

"I'll run a lemonade stand at the ball park," says one.

"I can help make the lemonade," says another.

"I'll water my grandmother's garden," says Marie. "She always pays me for that."

Albert walks in, and you describe your problem to him.

"I can cut wood for plaques and sell them to my aunt for her craft shop," he says.

Now everybody has committed themselves but you. You think really hard. There's only two things you do to make money for missions.

Choices: You start pony rides (turn to page 22).
You decide to do something entirely different (turn to page 130).

Setting the gazelle upon a shelf in your room, you step back to admire it. It does have the shape of a horse except for the head and antlers. You sit down to think about the missionary's list of needs:

- electric typewriter
- students' uniforms
- roof for chapel
- pastor's salary
- songbooks in native language
- sheets and pillowcases for hospital

Each evening you pray about these needs. Soon you become so concerned that you want to earn money for the missionary.

Choices: **You decide to start a pony ride in your backyard (turn to page 22).**
You decide to work on your uncle's ranch for the summer (turn to page 109).

The librarian helps you find a book that describes how to make the semblance of an Argentine bola. You ask the librarian to copy the article so you can purchase the materials and make the bola at home. She gives you this paper:

Argentine Bola:

Materials: 2 pieces of 30" clothesline
1 piece of 15" clothesline
3 rubber balls 2½" to 3" diameter

Directions: Poke a hole through each ball the entire length of diameter. Insert an end of rope into each ball. Tie free ends of rope into huge knot.

To Use: Seek an inanimate object, such as a post or telephone pole, as a target. Swing rope and balls above the head in a large circle. When speed is consistent, throw at object.

"That sounds tricky," says your friend.

"Ah, it's easy," you insist.

"Your mom won't let you make a bola. It's a dangerous weapon."

Choices: **You make a bola (turn to page 123). You forget about bolas and go to Alvin's to go horseback riding (turn to page 9).**

You find the rope and balls in a variety store. You purchase the rope even though you have twenty extra feet. At home you find that a screwdriver goes through the rubber balls and will push the rope through. You tie the ends of the rope on each ball to prevent them from slipping out.

Outside you practice until you seem to be able to control the bola. Some friends come over and you show your new bola to them. They want one, too. You figure out the cost of the rope and sell them the right amount.

Your best friend, Albert, constructs a bola for the inside of the house with soft Nurf balls and softer cord. One of the girls uses some Styrofoam balls and ribbon.

You practice throwing the bolas. All of a sudden you lose control of your bola and the weapon flies toward Albert.

He ducks. But the close call frightens you. You decide to make a bola like Albert's. Nurf balls won't hurt anybody, and they're still fun to throw!

THE END

Finally the day arrives. You are very nervous and excited. You have just called the vet to come to deliver your colt. Two hours later the vet shakes your hand.

"Your mare is the mother of a very fine filly."

You watch the filly eat her dinner and swish her tail. She has a spotted face that looks quite mischievous. During the next few days you hunt for the right name as you watch her frisk about. She shies at the cat and races across the paddock. Then she wheels around and chases the cat from Funny Bits's shed with fury.

"Clown," you chide her, "I ought to sell you to the circus."

She repays you by nipping your arm and stealing a handkerchief from your pocket. You feel quite ridiculous chasing her around the paddock, but you are afraid she'll try to swallow the cloth. As you finally corner her and retrieve it, you hear the guffaws of the vet who's come to check on his patients.

"That filly is hilarious!"

"That's what I'll call her," you say and write Hill-Lair-E-Us on the registration form.

The vet laughs again. "That's certainly an unusual name. She just may live up to it in **THE END.**"

At first Funny Bits is very nervous about pulling a sulky cart. She dances around, zigzagging it all over the empty track. She tries to gallop to run away from the cart and turns it over. Malford is skinned up some, but he's not concerned.

You don't agree. "I'm not sure Funny Bits is made out to be a harness racer. She might hurt you seriously before she learns."

"Give her time," says Malford, "and she'll learn to pull it. Then we'll beat everybody! You just watch. She's a very fast horse."

You go home. You cannot bear the sight of your horse fighting that silly little cart. Several days later Malford asks you to come and observe.

"Funny Bits is a pro," he says proudly.

Malford seems to be right. You clock them to compare their time with the winning times you've been reading about in the horse magazines. Funny Bits is quite speedy, so you enter her in the Bane County Fair sulky race.

Everything goes well until Funny Bits enters the ring with other racing sulkies. The sight and sound of all those detested carts around her makes her go berserk. She is taken out of the race.

Choices: You decide to enter Funny Bits in a horse show (turn to page 74).
You decide to retire her (turn to page 44).

You turn away in tears. You have one more question. "Did the foal die, too?"

"Yes," said the owner. He pushes Funny Bits's corpse to one side, and you see a lump beside her. "We tried to save it. The vet said the foal never breathed." He brushed his hand across his face. "Horses are like people to me. When I lose one, I grieve as if it were a close friend."

You feel tears welling up in your eyes. You turn away and start walking to Funny Bits's old stall. You run your hand over the smooth, horse-worn feed trough and remember how much you cared for Funny Bits. The tears flow freely.

The detective comes up and you dry your eyes. "I guess I was wrong …" you start to say.

"Don't worry. My job is to investigate anything that seems suspicious," he says.

You go home and think about all the good times you had with Funny Bits. At least she had a good home and plenty of ground feed while you had her. You think you'll get another horse someday, but not right now.

THE END

It's just as you thought. Sissy's horse headed straight for home. When you get there, the horse is tied to a tree in the front yard.

"Children!" exclaims Alvin's mother. Alvin's little brother runs to her, leaving his pony unattended. You sit atop of Funny Bits, wondering what will happen next. Thank goodness, Alvin's used to watching the little kid. He grabs the pony's reins.

"Well, I guess I'll go home," you say. "This has been quite a day."

He nods. "I wish we'd made it to Duff's. Then we'd have really had a heyday."

"Yeah, I know. Well, maybe tomorrow." You turn Funny Bits around, but are stopped by Alvin's mother who catches the bridle.

"I understand my kids have kept you from practicing polo at Duff's."

"Well, yes," you admit.

"Then I'll keep them, and you two can go to Duff's tomorrow."

Alvin lets out a whoop of joy. You are both glad that your baby-sitting has come to **THE END.**

When you get home you find you are still miserable. The preacher's warning to obey God seems to burn inside you more and more.

You go to bed, but sleep refuses to come. You keep tossing and turning until you decide to get up and get a drink of water.

The water doesn't help any, but you see your Bible lying on the nightstand. You open it up and these words leap out at you. "I tell you, no! But unless you repent, you too will all perish." (Luke 13: 3)

You kneel at your bedside and ask God's forgiveness. A peace comes over you, and you crawl back into bed to sleep soundly. The next day you're in the kitchen trying to figure out your tithe.

Turn to page 79.

When everyone leaves, you do your chores, taking care of Funny Bits's needs. Then you go into the house and try to think how you can earn the money.

"What's the matter?" asks your mom coming into the room.

"Ah, nuthin'," you say, trying to change the subject.

"Are you sick?"

You know she won't be satisfied until you tell her your problem, so you give in and describe the missionary project to her.

"You could run errands on Funny Bits like the pony express," she suggests.

The idea appeals to you.

"Or you could start a baby-sitting agency on Saturdays."

You are not so excited about the second idea, but you know there is more demand for this kind of work.

Choices: You decide to run errands (turn to page 113).
You decide to start a baby-sitting service (turn to page 116).

"OK," you say slowly. "I'll sell the colt." You know your parents won't let you keep two horses, but you would love to raise him yourself.

Malford seems to read your mind. "Don't worry, the colt has to stay with his mother for six months anyway."

Malford names a price that sounds good to you, so you sign the sales papers.

"I'll name him Bits 'n' Spots," he says. "He will be a good horse. His mother is strong and his father has speed."

You look at Funny Bits proudly. She's already on her feet, licking her colt from nose to tail.

"I'm so glad you're alive and well, Funny Bits. We'll have other colts, but I hope it won't happen again too quickly. You're all tuckered out." Funny Bits looks at you and seems to understand. She lets out a sigh and starts eating the bran mash. Both of you are glad the pregnancy has come to **THE END.**

Now even the leader is laughing. "Maybe you'd better help us by chasing the calf back into the chute, kid. You need to practice your horseback riding before you decide to rope."

For the next hour you run around after the calf while Chuck plays the rough-and-tough cowboy. It's dirty, tiring work, and you feel you've been mistreated, not only by Chuck but also by the leader. You think of your young people's group at church, where the leader and many of the kids help each other when someone has trouble learning a skill.

As you ride back home that afternoon, you decide that this roping club isn't for you. The morning certainly hasn't been worth lying to your parents. You are going to forget about becoming a champion roper and quit the club. You drop your lariat as you ride Funny Bits into your driveway, letting the rope trail out behind you to spell **THE END.**

"That is not Funny Bits," you tell the officer. "Look on my purchase papers. She was an Appaloosa, and this is a chestnut."

The policeman agrees with you. He turns to the owner who is looking scared.

"There must be some mistake," says the owner. "I'm sure this kid's horse died."

"I'd like to search your stables," you demand.

"Go ahead and search," he says. "I want to clear up this mystery myself."

You really don't believe him, but you go back inside the stables. The two men follow you.

Choices: You look in each stall (turn to page 134).
You go straight through the building to the paddocks beyond (turn to page 135).

You and Alvin visit each stall. Most of them are empty. A few are quite dirty. You grimace at the putrid smell. You are in such a hurry that you almost pass the thirty-second stall without looking in. Then you see a newborn, leopard Appaloosa foal beside a black mare.

"That's my horse," you tell the owner who has just caught up with you. "You've tried to dye Funny Bits black, but you couldn't change her striped hoofs or white-ringed eyes."

The stable owner tries to run away, but you trip him and tie him up.

"He has an accomplice," you shout to Alvin. "He's probably hiding down in the paddocks."

You're right. Malford is there. You're not doing badly for an amateur detective. Alvin manages to catch Malford off guard and knock him unconscious with a shovel. Then he calls the police.

Once the crooks are in the paddy wagon, you call your father to come and get Funny Bits and her foal. You can't wait to get them safely home. Your dream of owning a horse has come true— plus an added bonus. You are the proud owner of this beautiful Appaloosa foal. What fun it will be to watch it grow up!

THE END

Behind the stable you see Malford getting into a pickup that is hitched to a horse trailer.

"Stop that truck!" you yell at the policeman. "My horse and her colt are being stolen."

The cop tries to stop it, but Malford drives away. You listen as the officer uses his two-way radio to set up a roadblock at the main intersections in the area. Within the hour Malford is apprehended.

Funny Bits comes home with her brand-new colt, which you promptly name Funny Spots. You spend a lot of time watching the foal after school. Funny Spots learns to follow you around like a dog. When it's time to teach him to lead, he's so gentle that a tug on his forelock will bring him stepping daintily beside you. No one could love the two horses more than you do. You are sure you made the right choice.

THE END

You take money left after your 10 percent tithe to the tack store to buy something. As you walk around the store, you notice that the saddle you wanted to buy is on sale today. It's fifteen percent off.

"Am I dreaming?" you ask the clerk.

"No, that style is being discontinued. The manager wants to sell it quickly so he has the room to display the new ones coming in next week."

You buy it quickly, and still have money left over. You stop at the grocery and buy carrots for Funny Bits.

Funny Bits looks very sharp with the new saddle on her back. Within a week you begin a new business in addition to the pony rides. You take kids' pictures sitting on Funny Bits and sell the photos to their parents and grandparents for special occasions.

When the sales begin to dwindle, you search your mind for another creative moneymaking project. You do not want this to be **THE END.**

The man pays a good price for Funny Bits. You give your horse one last pat as you accept the check and walk away. It seems strange to be walking after you've ridden so much.

"Hey! Would you like a ride?"

You turn. A friend of yours rides up behind you on his pony.

"Where?" You kid him. "On the tail?"

"No, behind me. There's plenty of room."

You crawl on his horse behind him and ride double.

"Will you buy another horse?" he asks.

"Maybe."

"Don't you *want* another horse?" he asks. He is surprised you sold Funny Bits.

"Well, I don't know," you hedge. Now that you've owned a horse you realize what a lot of work and responsibility it is.

"You've got enough money to get a really good mount." Your friend is testing your attitude. "I have a cousin that has a sorrel for sale ..."

Choices: You decide to buy another horse (turn to page 105).
You're still not sure (turn to page 106).

You let each one crawl onto Funny Bits and take a turn riding at a walk around the block. The rider always sits tall in the saddle. He waves to each one on the ground as if he were Roy Rogers. Funny Bits obliges each with a great ride. Then you unsaddle and put Funny Bits back into the shed.

Everyone hangs around not knowing what to do next.

"Let's go play ball," someone suggests.

"Would you like to play ball?" asks Alvin.

"Sure," you say with everyone else. "Just let me get my glove."

"You can be the first to bat," everyone says.

"We'll make you the team's captain," says Alvin. Quickly the others agree. You know that they are honoring you, because you let them ride Funny Bits. It makes you feel good, but you know that Alvin has always been the team captain and first at bat. He is the best ball player in the neighborhood, and you've always been the worst.

Choices: You become captain and bat first
(turn to page 95).
You decide to bat first, but allow your friend Alvin to be the team captain
(turn to page 99).